GIRL SQUAD

KIM HOOVER

BELLA
B O O K S
2019

Bella Books, Inc.
P.O. Box 10543
Tallahassee, FL 32302

Printed in the United States of America on acid-free paper.

First Bella Books Edition 2019

Editor: Ann Roberts
Cover Designer: Sandy Knowles

ISBN: 978-1-64247-044-4

About the Author

Kim Hoover is a lawyer by training, a real estate entrepreneur by experience and a writer by nature. Raised in Texas, she spent three decades in Washington, DC, where she built her career and her family. She and her wife of twenty years raised two daughters there and now split their time between Miami and New York City. In her spare time, Kim is most likely curled up with a cup of coffee and her latest political advocacy project or philanthropic endeavor. She is a board member of Lambda Literary, Voices for Progress and Advocates for Youth.

Acknowledgments

I would like to thank my family for their endless support of me wherever my imagination has taken me. In particular, I would like to thank my wife, Lynn, for always believing in me, my daughter, Stephanie, for being my first reader and biggest cheerleader, and my daughter Lauren for being herself.

I would also like to thank the many friends who read early versions of this book, or just heard about it, and offered their approval and encouragement. You know who you are.

And finally, I would like to thank Ann Roberts, my editor, and all the women of Bella Books, who made possible the introduction of this book to the wider world.

For Mom
For Dad
Separate but Equal

CHAPTER ONE

May, 1973

"For Pete's sake, Carrie Ann, can you sit like a lady for once? You're too old to be acting like a contortionist at the Texas State Fair."

My mother had pulled me out of bed after midnight, throwing a robe at me and saying nothing more than "come to the living room." I obeyed, taking my usual place in the family circle—a swiveling velvet chair. I slumped down, my legs slung over the right arm, and my hands exploring the split-ended strands of hair that fell to my shoulders.

My dad sat nearby, his elbows on his thighs, his hands cradling his head. The television set, a heavy wooden console that sat next to the couch, flickered blankly, the fuzzy screen bathing him in light. I saw that he was crying. I looked at my mother, trying to read her expression. She was not crying. In fact, she looked happier than I had seen her in a long time.

"I said, sit up straight." She pointed a finger at me.

When she spoke, in that drawly voice of hers, my dad raised his head, glanced at me and straightened his back. "Leave her alone, Joyce, why don't you? She'll have enough to deal with after tonight."

I sat up at that, looking from one to the other. My mother pulled an upholstered wing-backed chair from the dining room and sat, perched on the edge like a blue jay assessing her prey. My dad let his head fall into his hands again while she primly folded hers in her lap, like a lady in church. When she spoke, I no longer recognized her voice. She was someone different, someone cold, emotionless, saying something that made no sense.

"Your father and I, we have decided to...to try a...to separate."

What? I jerked my head quickly in his direction. He stared straight ahead, not looking at her or at me, and giving no indication he had anything to add to her pronouncement. *What is happening?* My face burned hot with outrage, and suddenly, feeling as if everything I had ever known or understood about myself was all wrong, I jumped to my feet.

"Are you crazy?"

I stood toe-to-toe with my mother, towering over her with every scrap of energy I could muster, demanding a response. She sat perfectly still and remained silent. I fumed, my anger boiling to the point that I had to use all my willpower to resist slapping her in the face.

"You can't do this to me." By now I was panicked. "You can't get a divorce. How will we live? What will my friends say? What will your friends say?"

All I could think of was a long list of terrible things that would happen to me, like facing people at church as that girl from a broken home, or shopping at Goodwill because we couldn't afford clothes. The fear gurgled in my gut and I thought I might vomit.

"Calm down," she said.

I ignored her, and, recovering a little, bounded over to my father's crouched and cowering frame.

"Do something!" I demanded, my voice cracking and tears overtaking my face like a gushing fire hydrant. "Please, Dad."

He looked up and the desperation darkening his eyes crushed my hope of a solution. He was defeated. Whatever had happened between them had killed his spirit.

"Are you moving out?"

My tears had dried with the realization I had no option but to accept my mother's will. Hers was the strongest force that intersected with my life and I had long ago learned not to waste energy once her decision was clear.

"He's looking for an apartment," she said.

My attention snapped back to her. "Apartment? Where? I didn't know there were any apartments in this town."

"Yes. Even in this godforsaken town, there are apartments. There's a complex over by the Coronado shopping center. They have a pool."

I had never known anyone who lived in an apartment. Dumas was a small Texas town lined with rows of three bedroom/two bathroom, brick, one-story houses. I had a momentary vision of inviting my friends to a pool party over the summer. Then I banished that thought as I considered what my friends' parents would say behind our backs about that pitiable divorced man living like a bachelor. I slumped to my chair, gloom and dread covering me like a damp smelly blanket.

"Get to bed," she said, standing and signaling the end of this farcical family meeting.

"Where's Dad sleeping?"

"Mind your own business."

"In the guest room," he said, saying something at last.

He brushed past me, and I thought of saying something encouraging like "hang in there," or "you'll be fine," but I guessed he probably didn't want to hear anything like that right now.

As I stepped into my room, I saw a bright light shining onto my curtains from outside. I peeked from the side window and caught a glimpse of a man in a fancy car pulling away from our curb. But the distraction didn't last and I fell into bed with the weight of the world coming down on me.

Under the covers the tears came back, along with deep, hard sobs. I buried my face in the softness of my pillow, feeling sure no one in the world had it as hard as I did. No one had a mom as mean as I did or a dad as pathetic.

CHAPTER TWO

Two months later...

"Cal! Supper!"

I caught a glimpse of my mother standing on the front porch of our ranch-style house, looking up and down the block, squinting against the hot July sun. The summer was in full swing and I was enjoying the freedom of lazy days and keeping my own schedule. She waved me in as I came around the corner on my prized possession—a no-name-brand bike that I had tricked out to look like a Schwinn Stingray. My friend Rachel had the real thing, since her parents were willing to spend money they didn't have, but I had to save every penny for a whole summer to have enough to buy the banana seat and chopper handlebars fitted onto mine. The bike frame was not short and sleek like a Stingray, so it looked like a town car trying to be a sports car, but I didn't care.

I sped toward the house as fast as I could go. My long, dark hair slapped my face as it whipped in the high winds. I was late. I parked the bike in the garage and stepped over the grease spot left on the concrete floor by my dad's Chevy. A pang of guilt hit me because I rarely thought about him between our scheduled visits. Not having him around wasn't that different from when he lived with us. His work schedule meant he worked evenings and nights two thirds of the time. He had never made an effort to pay attention to me on the evenings he was home. And if he did say something to me, it was usually a complaint, a criticism, or an order. The only thing I can remember we ever really did together was watch the Dallas Cowboys on TV after church and maybe play a game of pickup football during halftime. That was fun.

Mom and I had fallen into a rhythm without him, not having to say too much to each other, knowing what our jobs were, almost like roommates. But I had crossed a line by being late for dinner.

I went straight for the silverware drawer, avoiding eye contact with her, hoping I could slide by without a tongue-lashing. I laid out the utensils on the table without saying a word. I held my breath, waiting for the bite.

"How many times have I told you—"

"I know! We had a team meeting after softball practice."

"It's no excuse," she said, putting a plate of chicken fried steak in front of me. "Supper is at five thirty and you know it. And anyway, why do you have to play that stupid game? You're a girl."

"It's girls' softball."

"It's not proper for girls to run around in the dirt hitting balls and yelling like hyenas."

There was no point in arguing. She sat across from me, her shoulder-length auburn hair pulled back and clipped at the nape of the neck. People had always said my mother was beautiful and now that I was fifteen, I could see it for myself. She dressed carefully, outfitted with earrings, necklace, bracelets, and scarves—just to sit down to dinner with me. She always wore lipstick and full makeup. She made her own clothes and mine too. She'd say, "Why buy from the store when I can make something better and cheaper?"

I glanced over at the empty chair where my father used to sit. Sure, I missed him, but, for the most part, I was fine with the way things were and my routine with Mom. This night, like most nights, we ate without speaking to each other. When I finished, I got up to go to my room.

"You clean up," she said.

"But I thought we were taking turns—"

"I said, you clean up."

"That's not fair!"

"Poor little Cal. So put upon."

She gave me the look that I called the hairy eyeball. I complied, even though we had a clear agreement that we would trade off cleaning up after supper and I had done it the night before. I slammed the pans around in the sink. I hated it when she used that "put upon" thing with me.

"Dang!" I screamed, smashing my finger accidentally as I brought the frying pan down with a thud.

When I had dried everything and put it all away, I picked up the telephone receiver that hung on the wall next to the sink and called Rachel.

"I'm coming over."

Rachel's mom opened the door. She was so different from mine. She didn't care that her house was a mess with piles of clothes all over the floor, even in the entryway. And she let Rachel get away with murder as far as cleaning up or doing her homework or going to church. Our moms had one thing in common, their looks. Rachel's mom had her hair piled on her head in a fancy do and she wore full makeup on her already gorgeous face. Her outfit was something she could have worn on a fancy date, but she always dressed that way.

"Oh, hi, Cal. Come on in. Rachel's in the living room." She stepped back to let me by, the ash of her cigarette firing as she sucked on the plastic tip.

Rachel waved my way without taking her eyes off the TV or removing the fork from her mouth. A frozen dinner teetered precariously on her knees. She was spoiled. She looked up at me and grinned like she knew what I was thinking, her bangs falling into her eyes, her freckled face framed by a pixie haircut.

"You think you're so cute," I said.

"Uh-huh."

"Can I make some ice tea?"

"Use the pan that's on the stove," she said, waving toward the kitchen.

I boiled water and poured it into a plastic pitcher over three Lipton tea bags. As the tea bags steeped, I felt the anger and frustration slip away. Rachel's house had always been my refuge. The place with no rules. The place I could run to when my house felt too heavy. Iced tea in hand, I flopped onto the couch next to Rachel, letting out a sigh.

"Have you been paying attention to this?" She pointed to the television and I saw it was a special news report on Watergate.

"Of course. I wrote our congressman a letter about it for an assignment in our typing class last spring."

"Did he write you back?"

"He did, but he didn't say much really. Said he didn't want to comment on something that was an ongoing investigation or something like that."

"I think he's a crook," Rachel said, pointing her fork at the TV.

"Adults really know how to mess up the world," I said, crossing my arms in disgust.

"What's your deal? Your mom again?"

"It's nothing really. You know her. We just get on each other's nerves sometimes."

"What's it about now?"

"Anything...nothing...everything."

"Well, you're the only one to take it out on now."

"I'm just glad we're leaving tomorrow for camp."

"I'm already packed!" Rachel said.

"Yeah, me too."

We stayed up until midnight watching reruns of *Perry Mason* while Rachel practiced making origami butterflies.

"What are you going to do with all those?" I asked, pointing to the messy pile of butterflies on the floor.

"I'm not sure," she said, giving them a loving look. "They're beautiful, aren't they?"

"If you say so."

"I've been thinking about getting a butterfly bush for the yard. I read about it in a magazine. I think they'd like that."

"You know they're not alive, dingbat. They don't have feelings."

"You say that, but how do you know? Why isn't it just as likely that a soul enters their body once they're finished and then they transform," she said with a flourish, her arms opening in a swoop to the ceiling while she gazed into the space above her head.

I looked at her blankly. I had no answer to that. Sometimes even I couldn't quite understand what went on in Rachel's head. I slept over and the next morning we drained glasses of Carnation Instant Breakfast before crossing the street to my house.

Mom drove us to the church to pick up the bus to camp. I slid the window down and felt the dry, hot air on my skin. Not many people had automatic controls on their cars and I was proud we did. I hung my arm out the window and closed my eyes.

"Don't wear that out," Mom said, frowning and pointing to the control button.

"Why? Does it run down the battery?"

"I'm sure it could."

I made a face at Rachel in the backseat like, "Oh boy, the battery could run down." She pretended to push her window button up. I laughed so hard I got the hiccups.

"Stop it, Cal," Mom said. "That's so unladylike."

She could kill my good mood faster than a lightning strike. I turned away from Rachel and stared out the window at the flat, treeless horizon. Just on the other side of the road, the wheat fields shimmered in the sun, giving the illusion of a watery wave undulating as far as I could see. I stared a little too long and it made me dizzy. We turned on Second Street and cut through block after block of brick, ranch-style houses on identical lots that made up that side of town.

A few minutes later we hit Main Street. We rolled past a row of one-story shops—a bakery, a drycleaner, a plumbing supply store, a food market, all places I'd grown up with. I had never lived anywhere else. The church rose on the corner at the far end of Main, its heavy façade dominating the block. Mom pulled the Buick into the church parking lot and went to the spot closest to the main door.

"Privilege of being Volunteer of the Month," she winked.

She taught Sunday school to fourth graders. Her regular job was part-time at an accountant's office where she did bookkeeping.

"Okay, girls," she said, giving us both a hug. "Be good."

"She's all happy chappy all of a sudden," Rachel said as we boarded the bus and got settled in back.

"That's how it is these days. One minute she's mad as hell. The next she can't stop smiling."

I glanced out the window to see if she was going to wave goodbye to us and caught a glimpse of her in the parking lot with a man I hadn't seen before.

"I wonder who that is?"

"Who?" Rachel said, looking over her shoulder.

"The guy talking to my mom."

He was tall and well-built with a shock of red hair.

"I don't recognize him," I said.

"Who knows?" Rachel said, turning her attention back to the group.

As the bus pulled out of the parking lot, I gazed at Mom and him for as long as I could. I lost sight of her just as, I could have sworn, it looked like she got into a car with him. And not just any car. It looked the same as the one I'd seen the night she dragged me out of bed to tell me about the divorce. I thought about it for a few miles, but before long, the gossip from school took over and I let it go.

The hottest story going around was about this new family who had just moved in over the summer. They were all the talk because they bought the biggest house in town. There were two kids—one boy our age and one girl older than us. The boys were all bug-eyed over the girl, Jane. They talked about her like she was some kind of beauty queen. All of us girls were getting worked up about hating her before we'd even seen her.

Word was she was coming to camp, but her mom was driving her because she didn't believe the church bus was safe. How weird, we all thought. Who would want their parents dropping them off like that? She sounded like a horrible spoiled brat.

CHAPTER THREE

That first morning, I tiptoed out of the girls' dorm and into the great room of the church's cabin. No one else was up yet. I had unsuccessfully tried to drag Rachel out of bed. I walked by the fireplace that dominated the room and out into the New Mexico summer. It was still cool before the sun came up. This was my favorite part of the day. I loved to see the sunrise.

"Look at that," I said out loud to myself as I sat on a rock ledge watching it come up that first morning.

"Hey," Rachel said, climbing up to sit next to me. "I'm really mad at you."

"What did I do?"

"You ruined my dream. I couldn't get back to sleep."

"What was the dream?"

"I was an astronaut. I was in Houston and I was about to be the first girl in space."

"Don't be mad at me. I didn't mean to."

"It was so real," she said, staring out at the desert.

"Come on, we'll be late for roll call."

As we walked back to the cabin for breakfast, we passed the outdoor amphitheater, the wooden benches rising up against a backdrop chiseled out of the red rocks and red dirt. We walked by buildings with classrooms for study sessions. And there was a canteen where, if you had some spending money, you could buy candy bars and Cokes.

"How do you get to be an astronaut anyway?" Rachel asked.

"Hmm. I'm not sure, but I'm guessing you probably need to be good at science."

"Shoot. I got a C last year."

"That's because you don't try. You didn't turn in your project on time."

"Right. But how did I know it was gonna ruin my chance to be an astronaut?"

"Yep. That was it. The only thing standing between you and a moon shot."

It took her a second to realize I was kidding. "You are evil, Carrie Ann."

"Don't call me that!"

As we walked through the prayer garden, I heard someone coming up from behind and turned to see who it was. I caught my breath. Oh my god. *That's her. Jane.* My stomach felt like I'd swallowed one of the nearby cacti. Why was I so nervous all of a sudden? My throat tightened up. I was dying for water.

"Hey," she said.

"Hi." My voice sounded strange and I just stood there, staring at her like an idiot.

"You must be Jane," Rachel said.

"And you are?"

"I'm Rachel. She's Cal."

I noticed her clothes right away. They looked expensive and not like anything you could get in Dumas. I understood why the boys had been so loopy over her. She was different from the rest of us, that's for sure. She was almost too perfect, even the way she stood there with her purse over her shoulder, her outfit put together just so, like someone you would see on the cover of a magazine.

"Where are you off to?" she asked.

"It's time for roll call. Aren't you coming?"

"Is that a Bible?" she asked, ignoring my question and pointing to my clutched hand.

Before I could stop myself, I said, "*Good News for Modern Man.*" I could see she had no idea what I was talking about. "You know, *The New Testament*. In modern language?"

She stepped closer and held my eyes so long I had to look away. "Do you buy all that?"

I paused, backing up, thinking, maybe for the first time, about whether there was any choice. "Are you asking if I believe in the Bible?"

She sat down on a stucco bench and motioned for us to join her. She pulled a pack of cigarettes from her purse and lit one. I gasped and exchanged a wide-eyed glance with Rachel, shocked at how bold she was.

"Want one?" she asked.

I shook my head, looking around to see if anyone else was coming, my heart beating rapidly. Rachel just sat there with her mouth hanging open. We sat silently, me worried about her getting caught smoking.

"I've never been to a Bible camp before," she said.

"Do you like it?" *Why do I care? Don't be such a geek.*

She raised her eyebrows and leaned back against the bench, crossing her legs. Her thighs flexed at the hem of her skirt and I noticed how muscular her legs were. I must have stared a little too long.

"Soccer," she said.

"What?"

"I play soccer. That's why I have these quads."

"Oh, sorry. I didn't mean to stare."

"It's okay. I'm used to it."

How stuck up.

"My father thought this camp would be a good way for me to meet some kids before school starts again since we got here so late."

"I see," I said, now just wondering how we could get away from her without being rude.

"He says these churches are the center of social life in a small town, especially in Texas. And hey, don't be disappointed."

"I'm…what? What do you mean?"

"I can tell this stuff means a lot to you." She waved her cigarette hand in a circle.

I turned red. I could feel it. *Is she making fun of me?* I wanted to change the subject. It was as though Rachel read my mind when she jumped in.

"You're not from Texas, then," she said, more of a statement than a question.

"I was born in California. We lived in LA until I was in fifth grade. Then we moved to Houston, now here. My dad's in the oil business. He's a petroleum engineer."

She said it so matter-of-factly, like it was normal to have an engineer for a father.

"Wow," I said, wondering what California was like, or even Houston. "But why here?"

"He got hired to run some big project. Something about a petroleum reserve. I'm not really sure what it's about, but it's a big deal. I guess I'll be stuck here through high school. Unless I decide on boarding school."

She blew a plume of smoke into the air above her head. Boarding school—one more thing I couldn't imagine. I wasn't even sure what it was, exactly. But I wasn't going to show it.

"Boarding school. That would be cool," I said, trying hard to sound like I knew what I was talking about.

"It's in upstate New York. My mother went there."

"What's it like? Have you ever been there?"

"I visited last year on spring break. I have to decide soon if I'm going to go there."

We sat in silence for a minute or two as she finished her cigarette.

"So," she said, "are you doing this Santa Fe thing?"

"Yeah, we always do. It's great. You get to bargain with the Native Americans. They have all their stuff laid out on blankets around the square. You should go."

"It's a date," Jane said, touching my knee as she stood up to leave. "See you later."

Don't go! I watched her walk, her sandals clicking on the stone walkway. Her blouse lifted in the wind and I saw her bare back. A rush went through me, like a flock of birds just took off from the middle of my stomach.

That night after dinner and cleanup, we all got together in the great room in front of the fireplace. The Youth Minister wanted to do a music talent show and encouraged anyone who could sing or play an instrument to come up to the front. Several kids came forward who could play piano, acoustic guitar, and conga drums.

I played the clarinet, but this was no place for that. I had taken guitar lessons for a while, until Mom decided she didn't want to spend the money or time driving to the teacher's house. I still practiced on an old one I picked up from a pawn shop, but I was too shy to play in front of a crowd. The Youth Minister knew I had been working on it, though, and he called me up.

"No!" I panicked. "Not by myself."

"I'll play with you," someone said.

It was Jane, who was making her way to the guitar stands and looking over the options. My heart was beating so fast and hard that I thought I was going to pass out. I was lightheaded as I walked toward the front of the group.

"Here," Jane said, handing me one of the guitars, "you play rhythm."

I fumbled with the strap, my hands jittery as I sat in a chair next to her.

"Just follow my lead," she whispered into my ear as we set up.

We played folk songs while the singers, and there were lots of them, took turns leading or going solo. I managed to keep up with Jane, strumming chords and feeling more confident with each song. She would look at me every so often, nodding and smiling like she approved.

"That was so cool," I said, stealing glances at her as we put everything away for the night. "How did you learn to play so well?"

"My mom," Jane said. "She plays."

"Wow. She taught you herself?"

"She stuck a guitar in my hand when it was bigger than I was."

"I'm jealous."

"I could teach you…if you want."

"Really? But you don't have to."

"I want to. You've got potential," she laughed.

"Oh, yeah, right," I laughed. "We could go on the road and sell out shows."

"You never know…" She tweaked my nose, sending stars swimming in front of my eyes.

"Hey," Rachel said, joining us. "Do you want to do s'mores out by the firepit?"

"You go ahead," Jane said, "I'll see you in the morning."

"Hey!" I called.

She turned to look at me.

"Thanks. Thanks again."

She winked and walked away.

"Cal," Rachel said as we sat roasting marshmallows by the fire. "What's going on?"

"Going on?"

"With that girl. Jane."

I might have paused for half a second before I said, "I don't know what you mean."

"You're acting all…googly or something."

"Just because I'm being nice to a new girl doesn't mean I'm googly."

She gave me a look that said you're full of it.

"Stop," I said.

Rachel didn't say anything else, but I knew she was right. Something about Jane made me feel…shaky, off balance. Not like my normal self. I'd only known her for a day, but I got a weird hollow feeling when I thought about her. I didn't want to talk to Rachel about it. I didn't understand it. I wanted to push it away and pull it back at the same time.

CHAPTER FOUR

The Santa Fe trip had always been my favorite part of the New Mexico visit. We loaded up on the coach bus for the twenty-five-minute ride into town. Everyone spilled into the street with orders to report back to the bus in four hours. That was enough time to wander, have lunch, and shop for trinkets the Native Americans sold on the square. I grabbed my sunglasses out of my bag. It was so bright I couldn't open my eyes without them. The locals set up shop on the sidewalks, mostly under awnings or roofs, to stay out of the sun. I counted my spending money. Just enough to buy one or two souvenirs.

"What do you think?" Rachel asked as we surveyed the possibilities.

"I've got my eye on this," I said, picking out a beaded leather coin purse with a zipper. The cream-colored leather felt soft in my hands. The beads, sewn in the shape of a headdress, were typical Indian colors—red, yellow, turquoise, orange.

"How much?" I asked the old woman seated in a wooden chair at the edge of the blanket.

"Five dollars," she said, without looking up at me.

"I have three."

The woman turned away, silent.

Jane joined us on the sidewalk.

"Well?" she asked.

"I'm bargaining," I whispered. I put the purse back down on the blanket and started to walk away.

"Cal's good at this," Rachel said proudly to Jane.

"Four-fifty," the woman said.

"I'll pay four. That's it," I said as I glanced over at the same selection of purses on the blanket next to hers.

The woman wrapped the purse in tissue and took the four dollars.

"Nice job," Jane said.

We walked down the row of blankets, looking over the trinkets, jewelry, clothes, scarves, toys, and games. Jane picked out a turquoise ring for her mother and a peace pipe for her younger brother.

"I hope he doesn't use this as a bowl," Jane laughed.

I didn't get the joke and looked at Rachel, who shrugged and started laughing anyway.

"How about lunch?" Jane suggested. "I'll buy."

"Sure," I said, thinking how easy it was to get used to a friend who had money.

"No thanks," Rachel said. "I'll just get something from the grocery store…like we always do."

She said *always* loud and in my face, and then she glared at me.

"Really?" I said. "What's wrong with doing something different for a change?" I said *different* loud and in her face.

"I don't want to do something different. I want to do it the way we always do."

"Well, fine. I'm going with Jane."

"Fine," Rachel said and turned away.

"I didn't mean to cause a problem," Jane said as we watched Rachel go.

"Don't worry about her. She'll get over it."

"Are you sure? Seems like you two have a routine going. I don't want to mess that up."

"You're not messing anything up. It's fine. Really. Let's go."

We found a small Mexican café on a side street and sat at an outdoor table in the courtyard. I wasn't used to ordering in restaurants since my family almost never ate out. And if we did, it was either a cafeteria or a drive-thru. I started to sweat a little as I looked over the menu. I worried that I'd look like a doofus in front of Jane if I didn't order the right way.

I glanced at her and she looked back with a playful smile. How hard could it be? I settled on tacos since I was pretty sure I knew what would appear on the plate.

"Was it hard leaving your friends in Houston and moving up here?" I asked.

"Oh, not that hard. With my father's job, we know we can move on short notice. So I guess I never get that attached to one place."

She lit a cigarette and smoked while we waited for our food.

"Still, you must have friends who you miss. I can't imagine moving away and not seeing Rachel almost every day."

She paused, drawing on the cigarette. "There was one girl… We got really close. But…" She crushed her cigarette in the ashtray. "It didn't really work out in the end."

"What do you mean?"

"My parents didn't approve of her."

"Why? What didn't they like?"

Jane looked away from me, away from the table.

"They said we spent too much time together and it wasn't healthy. That people were starting to talk about me and her."

"That's terrible."

"It's one of the reasons we moved."

"You're kidding."

"It's crazy I know. My parents get these ideas in their heads, especially my mom. She freaks out sometimes. She pressured my dad to find something that would take us away from Houston."

"Parents can be so selfish."

"Mine are hot and cold. Most of the time they don't care what I'm doing as long as I'm not embarrassing them."

"So they were embarrassed by something about you and this girl, but I don't understand what it was. Did she get you in trouble? Drinking? Sneaking out?"

"No, nothing like that. It's not worth talking about. I'm sorry I brought it up."

"Don't be." We sat for a minute or two without talking. The silence started to weigh on me and I worried she'd lose interest if I didn't come up with something. "Speaking of embarrassing, my parents got divorced this summer."

The waiter arrived and set our plates down.

"Oh, wow," Jane said. "Is it tough?"

"I hate it." I took a bite of taco. "I mean, it's not like I'm crying every day or anything. It's more like, I don't know, like I'm ashamed or something."

Jane nodded. "I get that."

"It just doesn't happen around here—the whole 'broken home' thing. Like there's something wrong with us."

I felt the heat on my face as it turned red. I hadn't talked to anyone except Rachel about this. And here I was talking to someone I barely knew.

"That sounds hard," Jane said. "I've had a lot of friends whose parents are divorced. Especially in California. But things are so different here. I saw that right away. 'Small towns, small minds,' my grandmother used to say."

"Yeah," I laughed, thinking of all the church people sitting in their pews with tiny heads. "I don't know. It's just… It's weird to think about my mom being single. I mean, you know how it is. Your mom is just your mom."

"Is she dating?"

"No. Why? Who would she date?"

"I don't know, but she's so young. I'm sure she wants to meet someone," Jane said.

"What do you mean she's young? Did we talk about that?"

Jane shifted in her seat. "Oh, uh, well no, I guess we didn't, but I think my mom heard something from somebody—"

Somebody said something? Who would say something? And why to Jane's mom? I felt like a knife slashed through my chest, heat spreading from the wound. Shame. It would never have occurred to me that people like Jane and her parents would gossip about me and my mom. More shame. Humiliation flooded over me. I couldn't stop it. I wanted to. As much as I wanted to stay and keep soaking in the attention from Jane, I had to leave. I got up and looked for the way out. Tears were coming. I didn't want to cry. I didn't want these strangers to look at me. I fumbled for the exit. I forgot my stuff, but I couldn't go back.

"Cal!" Jane stood and called after me. "I'm sorry! Come on, don't leave. Please."

As much as I wanted turn around and go back, I couldn't. I pretended not to hear her. I kept my head down and walked as fast as I could, looking for a place to hide for a while. The tears finally came, streaming down my face and soaking the collar of my shirt. I ducked into an alley. I wouldn't be able to take it if I ran into anyone else I knew. I found a covered bus stop and sat on the bench, not making eye contact with anyone. I tried to make sense of what had just happened. It hit me so fast.

People were talking about Mom. *Of course, they are.* She could do something like that and no one would say anything? Throw her husband out for no good reason? People didn't get divorced. Women didn't live on their own. At least not in our town. Ever since the night she told me, I had been acting like she and I lived on our own planet where the normal rules didn't apply. But Jane was right. Mom was only thirty-four. So what was she going to do with the rest of her life? She must have a plan. She wasn't the type to strike out on her own. She had never been on her own. She'd gone straight from her parents' house to my father's house.

How stupid I had been not to realize that there had to be a darn good reason why my mother left her marriage like it was nothing. That car I'd seen that night. The same car she got into with that man. That had to be it. My heart pounded in my ears as I let it sink in. She did have something—or someone—lined up. But why did she keep it secret? Who was he? What would happen to me in all this?

I kept my eye on my watch since the only thing that could make this situation worse would be to miss the ride back. When it was almost time to meet the group to go back to camp, I headed over. I slipped onto the bus and went straight to the back without looking at anyone.

Jane made her way to the back and sat down beside me. She opened her mouth to say something.

"Please," I said. "I really don't want to talk about it."

"I just want to say I'm sorry. I didn't mean to upset you."

"I know that. It's not you."

"Here," she said, handing me my bag. "You forgot this."

"Thanks," I replied, but I didn't look at her.

She took my hand and held it in her lap. My heartbeat pounded in my chest and sweat broke out on my forehead. I tried to pull my hand away, but she held on. When she finally let go, I slumped back into the seat, my eyes closed. My brain throbbed against my skull. Tacos churned in my stomach. I felt one of my sick headaches coming on and hoped I could make it back without puking in the bus. I got lucky—I fell asleep.

CHAPTER FIVE

Rachel was waiting for me as I got off the bus behind Jane. "I'm sorry for acting like a jerk in town."

"That's okay. I knew you didn't mean anything by it."

"What happened? You look like a truck ran over you."

"Let's take a walk," I said, waving goodbye to Jane.

We didn't say anything until we got away from the others.

"I've been so dumb."

"About what?"

"Something Jane said made me realize people around town are talking about my parents' divorce. And you know why? Because it doesn't make any sense. Not for a woman like her. Have your parents said anything?"

"Not a word."

"Why would my mom divorce my dad? What if there's someone else? Do you think that's it?"

"Why don't you ask her?"

"Are you kidding? Do you think she would tell me if there was? You know she won't talk to me about anything personal."

"I guess that's right. Maybe we should spy on her."

"I don't know if that's a good idea. Let me think about it. If she caught us, she would kill us."

Rachel gave me a hug. "You're my best friend," she said. "Always."

In the dorm that night, I noticed Jane settling in with the older girls at the other end of the room. She looked up and caught my eye at one point and smiled. The flutter went through me again and I looked away.

The next day, she found me at breakfast and wanted to apologize again for bringing up the gossip about my mom.

"No, I apologize for acting like such a weirdo," I said. "It just caught me by surprise. I've been living in my own little shell since it happened. Almost like Rachel and I were the only ones who knew about it. It was dumb."

She convinced me to start meeting in the prayer garden to practice guitar. It helped me get my mother off my mind. Jane wasn't very interested in Bible study or really anything going on at the camp, and we started skipping most classes so we could hang out together and play music, which wasn't like me. I was the one who always showed up with notes on the lesson, so prepared everyone made fun of me for it.

After a few days of this, Rachel confronted me. "Camp is always you and me, but all of a sudden, it's like you're not even here."

I looked away and couldn't think of anything to say.

"Why are you spending so much time alone with Jane?"

"It's the guitar," I said, a little too quickly. "She's teaching me."

"Is she your new best friend?" Rachel said with arms crossed and eyes narrowed.

"No, it's not like that."

"Well, then what is it?"

"You're my best friend. You'll always be my best friend. I love you."

Rachel smiled. "You better. Can I come to the prayer garden with y'all then?"

"You don't have to ask permission."

Later that afternoon, after Jane and I had played every song we knew, the three of us lay on our backs in the dry hot desert sun. Jane broke off a piece of cactus and wiped the oozing liquid from the broken stem to a cut on her elbow.

"It's aloe vera," she said.

"I know," I said. "That stuff grows on my grandmother's farm."

"What farm?"

"It's outside of Sweetwater, near Abilene."

"A ranch in the family!"

Rachel laughed, shaking her head. "It's mostly red dirt and tumbleweeds."

"You've been there? I'm jealous. How big is it?"

"She always says it's half a section," I said, "whatever that is. Somebody leases most of the land and runs cattle on it."

"I can only imagine…" Jane said, gazing off as if visualizing every detail.

"When I was a kid, I used to spend the whole summer there every year. Just me and Grandma." I closed my eyes, remembering. It was the smells that stood out—the stinky cow patties, the freshness of the hay bales, especially after a rain, the sour smell of cattle feed.

"What was it like?" Jane asked.

"We had our routines," I said. "On Saturdays we'd go to the library in town and get a stack of books for the week. Mondays were grocery shopping day. And I had chores. I had to feed the chickens every morning."

"I'd love to see it," Jane said, sitting up with her arms around her knees.

"Why?" I asked, squinting in the sun to look at her.

"It's just so Texas," she said, twisting her hair around her finger as she looked off toward the mountains in the distance.

She jumped up and extended her hands to me and Rachel, pulling us to our feet. On the walk back to the cabin, I fantasized about taking Jane to my grandmother's farm. I imagined walking her to the creek, crossing it and heading up to the pasture to check out the cows. I had walked it dozens of times with my mother and grandmother. Jane would be impressed. The story developing in my mind was interrupted as I came into the cabin door.

"You're on KP tonight," the Youth Minister said, pointing to a bag of corn ears to be shucked.

Jane and Rachel ran the other way before I could rope them in.

The last few days of camp flew by and before we knew it, the last night arrived, and with it the final performances of the entire camp. Jane and I had decided to play and sing a song we had written. The group gathered in the amphitheater with the 150 kids and adults who had been there over the two weeks. I was so nervous my hands were shaking, and they were so sweaty I wasn't sure I could hold onto the guitar.

"I don't know if I can do this," I told Rachel as Jane and I stood off to the side, waiting to go on.

"You'll be fine," Rachel said, clasping her hands together in excitement as if she were the stage manager.

"What if I forget the words?"

"I taped them to the floor." Jane pointed to a spot in front of the microphone.

"Oh my gosh," I said as Jane dragged me onto the stage.

The performance was mediocre since we stepped on each other's words and missed a few transitions, but the two of us were having such a great time that the crowd really got into it and cheered us on. As we left the stage, this feeling hit me, a feeling like I was about to lose something—like I better take this all in and not ever forget it. This had been the most amazing two weeks, but the next day we would head home, to the routine of an ending summer and eventually back to school. I felt almost sick at the thought of not seeing Jane every day. We would be at the same school in the fall, but juniors and sophomores did not cross paths much.

"Y'all go on," Rachel said. "I told them I'd help put away all the equipment."

As we walked under the stars on that moonlit night, the coolness of the desert chilling our skin, Jane put her arm around me.

"I'm going to miss you, kid," she said, hugging me close.

"Yeah, I was just thinking that."

We walked several steps arm in arm and then Jane stopped and faced me. She got really close.

"Will you call me?"

Something about the way she looked at me made me feel dizzy. I had to swallow before I could find my voice. "I'd like to," I whispered.

"Okay, then." Jane smiled. "I'll wait to hear from you."

On my way to breakfast the next morning, I looked for Jane, but I couldn't find her. I looked everywhere, feeling silly and panicked at the same time. I didn't want to act like I was obsessing about it, but I had to know where she'd gone.

"Oh, her mother picked her up early this morning," the Youth Minister said. "Something about soccer camp in Arizona."

It felt like someone pushed me off the side of a mountain, like there was no ground under my feet. Why hadn't she said anything? My brain scrambled my thoughts. She could have at least told me I wasn't going to see her on the ride home. How could she do this to me? Suddenly I felt like the past two weeks had been a fantasy. It didn't really happen. Maybe I made it all up. The tears were coming.

I ran to the girls' restroom and into a stall. I couldn't stop crying, and it was all I could do to stay quiet enough to hope no one could hear me. Finally, I came out and washed my face.

"What is wrong with you?" I said out loud, looking in the mirror. "Get over it!"

I had a hard time making conversation on the ride home. My head was spinning. *Jane, Jane, Jane.* I couldn't stop thinking about her. Rachel gave up trying to talk to me. She knew I was obsessed with Jane and that she'd disappeared on me. I think she felt sorry for me. Eventually, I was hypnotized by the passing landscape as the bus made its way back to Texas, red dirt and mesquite trees dancing in the desert heat. But I couldn't shake the unsettled feeling that gripped me and kept me off balance all the way home.

CHAPTER SIX

By the time August rolled around, with the beginning of school looming, I stopped thinking about Jane so much. This year was especially exciting since Rachel and I were finally in high school. It was still a few weeks away, and the school had sent us our schedules in the mail. I spent hours and hours going over the details of my classes, the names of the teachers, and studying the map of the building. I called around to find out which teachers were nice and which were tough. I wanted to be ready.

"You must have memorized that thing by now," Mom said over breakfast one Sunday morning before church as I looked at the schedule again.

"I have," I said, smiling and tucking it back into the front of my new calendar notebook.

She rolled her eyes, but I didn't care. So what if she didn't get me?

"I guess you're proud of that."

I ignored her and finished my breakfast.

"Did you see this?"

She pushed a letter across the table. It was addressed to me.

"You have been elected by the members of the boys' junior varsity football team to this year's JV cheerleading squad," I read. "Really? What am I supposed to do?"

"Well, sweetie, you're supposed to cheer," she said, the sarcasm revealing her annoyance. "The mom who is in charge called last night to say the boys picked you and five other girls to be their cheerleaders for the season. We have to design a uniform for you girls and you have practice a few times a week."

"When does this start?"

"I think they said the first practice is Tuesday night, and I guess I'll be spending my precious time driving you up there," she said.

Her agitation put me on edge and made me want to just drop the whole thing. What did I care about cheerleading? I hadn't done it since sixth grade. I probably couldn't do a cheer anymore anyway.

"I don't have to do it," I said. "I didn't ask for it."

"No, you're doing it. I'm not giving people in this town another reason to talk about my business. They do enough of that already."

"What are they saying?" I asked, surprised she would bring this up.

"It doesn't matter. But if word got out that I pulled you from cheerleading, it would just be an excuse to talk about what a bad mother I am."

"Who says you're a bad mother?"

"Your father for one. He went to a lawyer. Thinks he can get custody."

My stomach clenched. "Whoa, what?"

"Don't worry about it. He won't get anywhere. It's all about money anyway. He doesn't want to pay child support."

No way was I going to live with my dad. "But what could he say about you that's bad?"

"Nothing. Nothing he can prove anyway."

"Are you hiding something?"

"Watch it, Cal. Don't talk to me that way. Some things are for adults only. I told you not to worry about it."

"Will he have to pay child support?"

"He better. Otherwise, I don't know where I'm supposed to get the money for this uniform. And the shoes too."

I knew where this was going. I wanted to keep the peace with her.

"I'll help! I can get more babysitting. Don't worry."

"I might tell the other mothers I'll sew all the uniforms if they'll pay me. I could do it in a weekend."

"Thanks, Mom. I'm sorry this is so much trouble."

"Hey, maybe it'll improve my reputation with all these busybodies. I'll tell you what. None of them can sew a button on a shirt."

Mom and I got to church a few minutes early and she headed off to sit with the adults. I looked around for Rachel, since we usually sat together, but I couldn't find her. Her parents had probably let her skip again. Then as I turned a corner, I found myself face-to-face with Jane. In a split second, my heart pounded into the base of my throat so hard I thought I was going to choke. I hadn't thought about her in weeks. Now the memories of New Mexico rushed over me like ocean waves.

"Hey, stranger," she said, stepping toward me. She wore a top that clung to her figure and a skirt that was too short for church.

Keep it together . "Hi."

"You look so cute!" she said, arms open, inviting me in for a hug.

I stumbled and crashed right into her, almost falling at her feet.

"Thanks," I said, standing up straight and pushing my hair back out of my face. "So do you."

We stood there for a few seconds in silence. I wracked my brain, struggling for something, anything, to say.

"The last time I saw you—"

"Oh, I know. I should've sent you a postcard at least."

"No, I didn't mean—"

"My mom hijacked me. I didn't know she'd signed me up for soccer camp. I think she wanted to get me out of town for a while."

"Why?"

"We'll talk about it later. But, hey, I heard you're on the JV cheerleading squad."

"Well, yeah, I guess so. It was a surprise to me. How did you know?"

"My brother's on the team." She smiled. "He and the other boys think you're the best girl in the tenth grade."

I laughed at that. "Is that it? Well, I'm sure I won't be able to hold on to that title for long."

"Your mom must be proud of you."

"Ah, well, I don't know about that. She's not the least bit excited about hauling me around to practices and games."

The organ sounded the beginning of the service.

"Sit with me." Jane motioned to go in.

When she sat on the church pew, her skirt came up even further and I couldn't help noticing her thighs, still tan and muscular from soccer. I felt a little ashamed about how much I admired them. With my heartbeat thundering in my ears, I didn't hear a word of the sermon.

After the service, Jane pulled me into the side chapel. "I was thinking about your problem with a ride to practice."

"Okay," I said. "Why?"

"I just got my license, and I think I could convince my dad to let me use the car."

"To drive me? No way."

"I'm really good. I've been driving for a year. My dad thinks you should know how to drive once you're tall enough. He grew up on a farm and they were all driving tractors and trucks at fourteen."

"But why would you do it? The practices are twice a week, and, once school starts, we have games too."

"I'm sure I can't do all of it, but at least it's a chance for us to spend time together."

She wants to spend time together. But what if she disappears on me again? Like she did this summer. I don't want to get my hopes up. Get my hopes up for what? Why does she have such a hold on me?

"Hey, what do you think?" she asked impatiently.

"Okay," I said. "My mom won't care, as long as she doesn't have to be bothered with it."

I wasn't convinced she would show up, but sure enough, on the first night of practice, Jane pulled up at my house in her mother's Oldsmobile. I was waiting out front and ran to the car as she stopped at the curb.

"I can't believe your parents let you do this. Thank you."

"Hey, I told you I'd come through. And I get to watch you practice," she said, touching my knee.

"Oh my gosh." My stomach flipped. "I didn't think about that."

"Don't be nervous. I'm your biggest fan."

I could have sworn she blushed. "That's sweet," I said, suddenly feeling bold with her.

Jane sat in the bleachers with a few moms and a few boys who were watching practice. I felt self-conscious at first, but after a while I forgot she was there.

"What do you think of those other girls?" Jane asked as we drove back to my house.

"What do you mean?"

"Do you feel like you have much in common with them?"

"Well…hmm. I never thought about that. I've known them my whole life."

"All they're interested in is performing for the boys, making themselves up for the boys, dressing to get their attention. It's all so tiresome."

As the car stopped at my curb, she leaned her head back on the seat and let out a sigh of exasperation.

"I guess I never noticed," I said. "But you're right. So much eye shadow!"

"Makes you want to line 'em up and hose 'em down!" Jane mimicked a firehose trained on a line of girls. We had a good laugh thinking about it.

"You don't wear all that makeup. Why not?"

"I don't know. I just never got interested. My mom tried to teach me last year, but she gave up when I wouldn't put that mascara brush near my eyes."

"Well, you're very pretty without it," Jane said, smiling, her voice breaking a little.

My face felt like it had caught on fire. I had the strangest sensation of weightlessness as my gaze locked on hers. I caught my breath and opened the car door. "I better go."

Hey," Jane said as I got out of the car. "Do you want to sleep over on Saturday night? We can get pizza or something."

"Sure," I said, still breathing a bit faster than normal.

"Good."

"You're gonna think this is weird," I said, relaxing. "But I've never had pizza before."

"Hmm, I think there's a lot I can teach you, young Cal." She smiled and drove off.

CHAPTER SEVEN

Mom was in the kitchen when I walked inside the house. "Is that going to be a regular thing?" she asked.

"What?" I said, thinking about the "date" with Jane and wondering whether that's what she meant.

"Her giving you a ride."

"Oh, I'm not sure."

"Sure would be nice," she said.

"I don't know if she can always get the car, but I think she'll help out when she can."

"She's that new girl from the rich family."

I shrugged. "I guess so."

The phone rang. Mom dropped the pan she was fussing with and ran to her bedroom, almost pushing me out of the way as she went past. *Why didn't she just pick up the telephone in the kitchen? It was a foot away.*

I stared at the telephone hanging on the wall, thinking about Rachel's idea to spy on my mom. I hesitated, then held down the cradle hook and picked up the receiver. I released the hook slowly, so as not to make any noise. I held my breath, afraid they would hear me.

"I'll be gone for a few nights," a man said.

This had to be him. The man who had driven by our house that night. The man she'd slipped into the car with that day we left for New Mexico.

"Where this time?" Mom asked.

"Tulsa," he said.

"I'll miss you."

"Me too. We'll do something nice when I get back."

"Is Mimi going with you?"

"Nah, she's got things to do."

"That's good. I can't stand the thought of her being in your bed."

"You don't have anything to worry about there."

"Okay. Will you think about me?"

"Every second," he said. "Now let me go."

They said their goodbyes and hung up. My hand shook a little as I put the receiver back in the cradle. *Why don't I know about this guy? If she's dating him, why wouldn't she tell me?* So many questions. *Who is Mimi? What is Mom worried about?* Hearing her talk to him was so strange. Her voice was different. Softer.

When she came out of her room, she almost danced down the hall, humming and snapping her fingers. She called me to the dinner table. I looked at her for the first time, not as my mother, but as a woman. I couldn't help envisioning her with the man on the telephone. The man I had seen in the parking lot that day.

"What's wrong, Cal? You look like you've seen a ghost."

I tried to forget the image I had conjured of them in each other's arms. "Nothing. It's just…nothing."

She glossed right over it. "I forgot to tell you, your grandmother is passing through on her way to Ruidosa Downs."

"When?"

"Friday night. Too bad she can't stay, but it's better than nothing."

Good! Perfect timing. Grandma would want to hear my

theory on the red-haired man. She loved a good mystery. And it was no secret that she and Mom didn't see eye to eye on a lot of things. I couldn't wait to talk to her.

She arrived on Friday while I was at the city pool. She greeted me at the door when I got home.

"Your mother's gone off for a few days," she said, disapprovingly.

"What? Where?"

"Not sure," Grandma said. "Something about a conference."

"Why wouldn't she have told me?"

"I don't know, honey. Sometimes your mom is a very difficult woman to figure out." She took the stance she used when something didn't sit right with her—stiff, upright and with her arms crossed. "So, anyway, I'm here for the duration."

"Wait. I thought you were only passing through? What about Ruidosa?"

"I canceled that. I didn't think you should be here by yourself."

"You didn't have to do that. I'm spending the night with a friend tomorrow night anyway."

"It's okay. Lord knows I don't need to do any gambling. I lost my shirt the last time I was there."

"Grandma, I think I might know something about why Mom is gone this weekend."

I told her about the conversation I had overheard. "I think maybe she's with him."

"Very interesting indeed," Grandma said. "So now you're a detective?"

"Are you mad?"

"No. 'Course not. I don't blame you. I've been wracking my brain trying to figure out what she's up to. I never thought she'd get divorced until she had something else lined up."

"What should we do?"

"Nothin' to do right now. Just keep your eye out, the way you have been. She'll show her hand sooner or later. Now, let's have some fun. I bought TV dinners."

"Grandma, you're the best!"

We ate sitting in front of the television, breaking the house rule. Grandma let Rachel come over and eat with us. She even baked an apple pie, my favorite. After dinner, Rachel and I sat outside in the backyard, watching for falling stars.

"Rachel," I said as I turned to her and leaned in.

"Yeah?" Rachel leaned back toward me like a co-conspirator.

"There's something I want to tell you, but you have to swear not to say a word to your mom. Can you keep a secret from her?"

"Does a bird fly?"

"You know I've been wondering why on earth my mom would divorce my dad?"

"Yeah."

I took a deep breath and stared out into the night. "Well, I think my mother might be seeing someone, kind of on the sly."

Rachel stayed quiet, waiting.

"I don't know anything for sure, but her being gone this weekend doesn't make sense."

"Where is she?"

"I don't know. Grandma doesn't even know."

"How do you know she's seeing someone?"

I told her about the telephone conversation. "And she runs to her room every time the phone rings. Sometimes she's in there for half an hour."

"Well, couldn't she just have a boyfriend? I mean, grownups do that, don't they?"

"Yeah, but there's something sneaky about this."

"Don't worry about your mom. I'm sure it's fine. How much trouble could she get into in Dumas?"

"I guess you're right."

I went back inside where Grandma was putting away the dishes we'd all washed.

"When can I come to the farm?"

"You can catch the train in Amarillo any time you want. I'll pick you up in Sweetwater."

"Can I bring a friend?" I asked, thinking of Jane.

"Why not?" Grandma was always game for outside company. "The more the merrier."

"Remember that time Rachel came with me and she peed outside and got poison oak?"

"Oh, lord, that girl was on fire!"

We laughed, but poor Rachel had been miserable for a week.

"Mom was so mad. She told us not to walk on that side of the creek."

"She wanted to tan your hide, but I wouldn't let her. Let the girls explore, I told her."

"She hated me getting dirt under my fingernails."

"Well, she never did like you playing outside so much."

"Maybe it's that she just doesn't like *me*, Grandma."

She hesitated just a little too long before she said, "Don't be silly. She's your mother." Then, changing the subject, "So you want to bring Rachel for another visit?"

"I was actually thinking of inviting this new girl." As I said it, my heart started to beat a little faster and I looked at Grandma, hoping I didn't seem too excited.

"That's fine, honey. What's her name?"

"Jane," I said, my voice betraying me with a squeak.

"Somebody special, huh?"

I turned away from her. "Oh, not really. Just…She said she'd love to see a Texas ranch."

"Ranch!" Grandma let out a huge belly laugh. "Well, sounds like you may have built it up a little more than it deserves."

"See, she's from California, so she has this thing in her head about Texas, and you know…I just thought it would be fun to show her."

"Come here and give me a hug," Grandma said, and she held me tight. "Anybody you like, I like."

CHAPTER EIGHT

Jane's house reminded me of something you would see on a TV show. It sat on ten acres of land at the edge of town. With a stone and concrete columned entry and a long, paved driveway up to the main house and outbuildings, it felt like a separate world. I rode up the drive slowly, half expecting a guard to stop me and ask why I was there. The trees that lined the drive formed an arch over my head. There aren't a lot of trees in Dumas. It's so dry and almost like the desert, so who knows what they had to do to keep them alive?

I parked my bicycle near one of the four garage doors. As I walked across the drive, looking for a front door or some way to knock or ring a doorbell, Jane came around the corner. The minute I saw her, my legs went weak, my stomach started churning and I felt like running away. She wore a thin, white cotton dress that the wind pressed against her body in a way that outlined her bra and panties. Her hair tumbled past her shoulders in rich, brown waves. The now familiar rush of heat pushed through me. *Why did I feel so weird around her?*

"There you are," she said, hugging me tightly. "Sorry I couldn't come pick you up."

She smells so good! I tried to relax. *Don't say anything stupid.* "This place is…wow. I don't even know what to say."

"This is what happens when you move from Houston to a small town. Our house there was half this size. Come on," she said, reaching for my hand. "I'll show you around."

Even half this size would be three times the size of my house. There were six bedrooms and eight bathrooms. It had a service kitchen (I didn't know there was such a thing) with a huge butler's pantry and a dumbwaiter.

"My brother and I load this up with snacks and send it up to the third floor," Jane said, winking and pointing to the dumbwaiter. "Our rooms are up there."

Jane's bedroom suite had its own bathroom—as did all the bedrooms. It felt as big as our whole house. It was so spacious I could have done a few cartwheels across the floor.

"Let's go to the poolhouse. Did you bring your suit?"

Jane dug in a drawer and produced hers. I pulled mine out of my backpack. "Here it is."

"We can change over there."

We walked to the poolhouse and she showed me the private changing rooms and showers. The walls and floors were dark wood and there was a steam room and a sauna as well. The pool deck was made of the same stone as the house and had a rough finish so it didn't feel slippery. Plants and flowers decorated the space and garden lights shone on the statues that lined the perimeter of the deck.

"Watch this," Jane said, flipping a switch somewhere.

"Wow!" The pool came to life with strobes of different colors pulsing through the water. "I've never seen anything like this. It's unreal."

"It's a little over the top. My parents would never have built something like this, but since it was here, they thought they might as well fix it up and use it."

As I stepped out of the shadows and closer to the pool, Jane loudly whistled at me. "Wow! I had no idea you had such a great body."

"What are you talking about?" I grabbed a towel and wrapped it around me as fast as I could.

"Cal, c'mon. Have you looked at yourself?"

"Not really," I said, throwing the towel onto a lounge chair and jumping into the water where she couldn't see me so well.

She dove in and swam toward me, remaining underwater. *Like a shark.* She came up next to me, smiling and pushing her hair away from her face, then floating on her back, eyes closed. I couldn't help staring. She wore a skimpy two-piece yellow suit that stood out against her tan skin. The sun, slipping down the sky onto the horizon, hit the pool at just the right angle, so as she floated on the surface, her body shimmered in the last light of the day.

"I see you looking at me," she said, opening one eye in my direction.

I didn't stop looking. I looked even harder. She swam toward me, her head emerging from the water just inches away from me, beads of water glistening on her face. We stood, silent, in the shallow end of the pool, our bodies almost touching. I could feel her breath on my face. It smelled minty, like toothpaste. She touched my arm. I felt the most amazing throbbing between my legs and a lightness in my head. I waited, unsure for what, and unable to look away. She traced my lips with her finger. My whole body turned to goose flesh. She leaned forward and I thought she was going to kiss me.

The sound of metal scraping on stone startled us apart.

"Shit!" A boy said, tripping over a wrought iron chair. Jane dove for the pool ladder, climbing out at lightning speed.

"Goddamn it, Ted. Get out of here!" she shouted, grabbing for something to throw at him.

"You girls having a good time?" he said, smirking at me and giving me a look that made me want to grab the towel again.

"I'm serious, Ted. You are a dead man."

She came at him full force and was in his face, fuming something under her breath that I couldn't make out. He stood there for a few more seconds before he turned and left, calling out to me over his shoulder.

"See you later."

Jane sat down on the edge of the pool, her legs dangling in the water. Still in the water, I rested my elbows on the deck next to her.

"Jerk," Jane said. "Sorry about that."

I laughed. "It's no big deal. Why did you make him leave?"

"He and I have an agreement," Jane said, smiling.

I pulled myself out of the water and sat next to her "Agreement about what?"

Her eyes scanned me from head to toe before she responded. "I'll explain it to you someday...when you're older." She grinned and gave me a quick smack on the thigh before jumping up and grabbing a towel. "Come on," she said. "We have to get ready for dinner."

"I thought we were getting pizza?" I suddenly worried about the clothes I'd packed.

When we got back to Jane's room, she told me that her mother wanted to spend some time getting to know me and thought a family dinner would be the perfect setting.

"We have to be in the dining room in an hour," she said.

"Why didn't you tell me?" Disappointment swelled in my chest, like she had betrayed me somehow.

"I was afraid you wouldn't come," she said, looking away.

"You were right. You shouldn't have tricked me."

"It's not what I had in mind either," she insisted, pleading with her eyes. "But my mother wants to get a good look at you."

"Why?"

My anger softened as I realized she might cry, but I started to feel a little frantic about having to make conversation with parents like hers. And I really didn't know how I was going to get past the issue of what to wear.

"She always has to meet any girl I'm interested in."

Jane threw herself on the bed, hands over her eyes.

"You mean so she can make sure you're not getting in with the wrong crowd or something?"

"It's not that," she said, sitting up. "It's just that you and I have been together a lot lately."

"Wait," I said. "Are you saying this is like what happened in Houston?"

"No, that's not... Never mind. It doesn't matter."

"Well, I don't have anything to wear. I think I should just go home."

"No!" Jane jumped up and ran over to her closet. "Let's calm down. This is not a big deal."

She took a sundress off its hanger and held it up to me.

"This will work. And here," she said, handing me a pair of heels.

"Heels, really?"

"Just put them on. You'll be gorgeous."

When we came downstairs, Jane introduced me to her mother and father, Mr. and Mrs. Rawlings. Her father wore navy blue slacks, maroon loafers and a white knit shirt with an alligator on it. His neatly trimmed dark hair had flecks of gray sprinkled in. Her mother wore her dark brown hair in a tight bun, which accentuated her sharp features. Her gray linen suit with its white trimmed lapels and pocket flaps looked very expensive.

Jane and I sat next to each other, opposite Ted, to whom I was then formally introduced. Even though he was in my class, I hadn't actually met him before. The parents were on either end of the table. I sat rigidly straight in my seat, afraid to touch anything. Mr. and Mrs. Rawlings drank red wine, offering to let us try some. I said no, thinking I felt tipsy enough without trying to drink wine for the first time. Just sitting next to Jane was fogging my brain. A maid dressed in a uniform served the meal. I thanked the maid so often, Jane finally told me to stop.

The mood in the room felt oppressive, as though each of us occupied our own world. Even though Jane sat right next to me, she might as well have been in the kitchen. The intimacy at the pool had disappeared. *She's not all bravado after all.* When the maid brought out a brownie with ice cream for dessert, I was so relieved that it was almost over, I let out a little sigh. But that's when the questions started.

"How do you like being on the cheerleading squad, Cal?" Mrs. Rawlings asked.

"It's fine." No one else said anything, and feeling pressure to go on, I added, "I like the uniform."

"Really," Mrs. Rawlings said.

"My mother made it," I continued, feeling like an idiot, but not knowing how else to keep the conversation going.

"Made it?"

"She sews."

"Oh, I see." Mrs. Rawlings nodded. "I don't have domestic talents myself."

"It saves a lot of money. She made the other girls' uniforms too." Everyone's eyes were on me. "They paid her."

"Of course," Mrs. Rawlings said. "That worked out well."

"Jane says you play the guitar," I said, desperate to get the attention off me.

"Not so much anymore," she said, "but, Cal, tell me, do you have a boyfriend?"

Why is she so focused on me? "Not really. No one steady anyway." *Maybe she thinks I'm interested in Ted.*

"Well, I'm sure that won't last long. You are very attractive, Cal," Mrs. Rawlings said.

I swallowed hard and felt my cheeks burning. *Get me out of here!*

"Mom," Jane said, exasperated. "Please. Will you stop embarrassing her?"

"It's okay, Jane," I said. "Thank you, Mrs. Rawlings. It's very nice of you to say that."

"Yes, well, it's important not to waste your good looks while you have them," Mrs. Rawlings said.

I noticed how she cut a sidewise glance at Jane. *What's going on here?*

"Can we be excused?" Jane asked, looking pointedly at her father.

"Not yet," her mother responded before he could get a word out. "I have another question for our guest."

Now what? I sat quietly, waiting, feeling the anger seething from Jane's body next to me.

"You mentioned your mother, the sewing, saving money. I'm just wondering, how does she like being a single divorcee in a small town?"

"Are you kidding?" Jane was on her feet.

"Helen, that's out of line," Mr. Rawlings said. "I'm sorry, Cal. I think my wife may have had a little too much to drink tonight."

"Let's go," Jane said as she grabbed my hand and dragged me out of the room.

"What was that about?" I asked when we got back to Jane's room.

"She was drunk. I'm so sorry."

"I can't believe I went on and on about those stupid uniforms."

"You were fine."

"I was terrible. They think I'm a moron."

"They do not."

"What was that about me having a boyfriend? Does she think I'm after your brother or something?"

"No, she's just...old school. I don't know."

"What about you? Do you have a boyfriend?" I asked, raising my eyebrows.

"My mother hounds me constantly," she said, putting a record on the turntable.

"But do you?"

"I think you know I don't," she said, coming closer, brushing my arm with her hand. "If I did, wouldn't he be here?"

I felt dizzy and my lips trembled, vibrating with an energy of their own. The nearness of her body to mine caused confusion to overwhelm my thoughts and I had the strangest sensation. I wanted to kiss her. *What?* I was frozen, my feet stuck to the floor, my hands and arms immobile.

"Let's go out by the pool," she said. "Ted and I have some beer stashed."

She grabbed her guitar and my hand, dragging me out the door and down the backstairs. The air was cool and the sky was clear and full of stars. Ted had the firepit going at one end of the pool deck. Nearby there was a cooler full of Long Necks. Ted handed me one.

"Thanks," I said, determined not to let on that I'd never tasted beer before.

I sipped the beer, thought it tasted bitter, but managed to drink half of it. I didn't make eye contact with either of them as I slipped the bottle under my chair, out of sight. Jane was strumming her guitar, a cigarette smoldering nearby. She sang folk songs while Ted stoked the fire. I closed my eyes and soaked in the sounds of the fire crackling and Jane's soothing voice. The next thing I knew, Jane was shaking me awake.

"Hey, sleepyhead," she said, kissing me on the forehead. "Time for bed."

I woke up early and decided to sneak out of the house before I could run into anyone. I left Jane a note, thanking her for everything. I rode my bike through the main gate, looking back on their magical kingdom, wondering how I had been so lucky.

The smell of breakfast hit me as I opened my front door. Grandma was in the kitchen making her usual, eggs fried in bacon grease, grits floating in butter, and homemade biscuits. I swooned with memories of summers in her kitchen.

I sat on a barstool and asked, "Can we skip church today?"

"I don't have anybody I'm trying to impress here," she said. "Yay!"

She put a plate of food in front of me. "Your mom called and said she'd be home early afternoon."

My insides cinched up. What would I say to her? I had no idea what to say. Would I have the guts to confront her and ask her point-blank what was going on? She wasn't the type to have a heart to heart. She wasn't that kind of mom. She kept her distance, like she didn't really want me to know what she thought or how she felt, unless it had to do with how I slumped in a chair or didn't keep my room straight. It was hard to get her to talk to me about things you're supposed to talk to your daughter about—like periods or body parts. We didn't even have a name for vagina. We didn't mention it. Ever. So how could I possibly ask her if she had a secret boyfriend?

"Grandma, you know Mom better than anyone. She's likely to bite my head off if I say something about that guy, but I'm dying to ask her."

"Listen, gal. You're old enough to start standing up to her. I know it's not easy. She's got a hard shell. But she threw your daddy out, so you're more or less the second adult in this house now."

"I don't know about that."

"You know, I never wanted her to marry him in the first place."

"Why?"

"She was so young but she thought she had to get out of my house. Got married a week after high school graduation. I begged her not to."

"You didn't like him?"

"Had nothing to do with that. They just had no business setting up house at that age. Then they had you and they were an old married couple by age twenty. So no wonder she's got wanderlust by now."

"Did she want to have me?"

"Oh, honey, it's not like that. When you get married, you do your duty and sooner or later, the kids show up. She never thought it through. But I guess she figured her duty was done once you were born, since you're an only child."

She winked at me, but I didn't think it was funny. I was beginning to understand why I never felt like my mother really liked me. I was used to it, but it still made me sad. I put it out of my mind, like always.

We cleaned up the kitchen together, and suddenly I felt really tired, so I went to my room to take a nap. But I couldn't sleep. I kept thinking about Jane in the pool, so close to me I could have pressed every bit of myself against her. I wanted to be there again. I wanted to touch her everywhere. I wanted her to touch me. But why? I punched my pillow. Slapped my thigh. It was not supposed to feel like this. God absolutely did not approve of it. I knew that for sure. But that didn't change what I was thinking, how I felt, what I wanted. It just made me feel alone. Like something about me was not quite right. Like when you know there's something you have to do, but you also know there's no way you can do it. It's impossible.

I got up, looked at myself in the mirror, and Jane came right back into my head as I compared my looks to hers. Jane was more glamorous than me, for sure, and I thought she was prettier. My eyes were my best feature. They were hazel green like no one else's I'd ever seen. Brown mixed with blue. I'd heard it all my life, how unusual they were. I wondered if Jane had noticed.

When I heard Mom's car pull into the garage, I was grateful for the distraction. *I have to get out there.* I brushed my hair. I smiled at myself and took a deep breath. Grandma sat at the kitchen counter reading the Sunday paper. Mom came in carrying a small overnight bag that she dropped on the floor with a thump. She leaned against the counter, rubbing her temples.

"Hi, doll," Grandma said.

Mom half smiled. "Everything all right?"

"The kid and I held down the fort."

"Where were you?" I asked.

She scowled at me, winding up for a verbal punch. "None of your business."

"I saw you with that man."

I couldn't believe that came out of my mouth. When she answered me, her teeth were so clenched I thought she might chip one. "Don't you ever spy on me again! You don't know anything. And you don't need to know anything." She pushed past me, leaving Grandma and me shocked into silence.

Even for her, that was harsh. I felt very small. All my bragging about getting to the bottom of it had deflated to dust.

"Well," Grandma said, "I guess that's that. And since there don't seem to be anything more for me to do here, I think I'll go to Ruidosa after all."

She packed her things and gave me a hug. "I love you, kiddo. Don't worry about your mom. She's always figured things out and usually comes out on top. But if you need anything, you let me know."

As I watched her drive off, feeling like my lifeline was disappearing, a tear slid down my cheek.

CHAPTER NINE

Preseason high school football started two weeks before the beginning of class. Our JV squad had their first scrimmage against Pampa High School. The other girls were thrilled that the cheerleading squad would get to perform, but I was not in the mood. Cheerleading felt so trivial to me at this point, but when Jane told me she wanted to go to the game and drive me, I changed my attitude. I was out on the front porch waiting when she pulled up.

"Ready for show time?" Jane said, getting out of her mom's car with a camera in her hand.

"Don't you recognize my game face?" I grinned really big and held pompoms to my cheeks.

"I have to get a picture of this."

"Let's get one of both of us," I said.

Rachel came across the street to join us and took the camera from Jane.

"This is a nice camera!" Rachel said. She held the Nikon carefully.

"Dad brought it back from Japan."

"Of course he did," I said.

"Don't be mean," Jane replied.

"Y'all pose," Rachel said.

"I'll be the football player," Jane said, holding up her arm and making a muscle.

"Woohoo, well for sure we can't lose," I said.

"Hey," Jane said to me in a deep voice. "Whatcha doin' after the game?"

"Come on!" Rachel said. "We need to go."

When we got to the stadium, Rachel headed off to meet a group of sophomores. "Don't worry about me. I'll get a ride home."

Jane walked me down to the field and dropped me off where the cheerleaders were warming up. She climbed into the stands and sat with some other juniors near the home bench. I looked up at one point and noticed her talking to one of the senior boys, a basketball player who I knew had just broken up with his girlfriend. I couldn't stop watching them, wondering what they were talking about and whether Jane might think he was cute. When Jane turned away and waved to me, I smiled and waved back, probably a little too enthusiastically, because one of the other cheerleaders, Tammy, looked at me funny.

"Who's that?" she asked.

I turned back to the field, feeling guilty, like I had been caught. "Oh, she's somebody who just moved here. I know her from church."

I wondered if my voice sounded as strange as I felt. I hoped Tammy hadn't noticed. But why? Could she tell how anxious I was to know that Jane was watching me? That wouldn't be good. I forced myself to focus on the game, and I resisted the urge to look up at Jane every second. But at halftime, when we performed our cheer routine, my eyes drifted in her direction. She was watching me and only me. I felt that sensation again—a little breathless, my heart beating quicker than it should, a big smile breaking out as our eyes connected.

We hadn't made a plan for after the game, so when it was over, I took my time getting my things together, hoping she would come by for me. And she did.

"Hey," she said. "Some of the kids are going out for pizza. We should go."

I reached for my wallet and looked inside to find only a dollar.

"It's on me," Jane said. "Come on."

"No, I've got babysitting money at home. I'll pay you back."

At that moment, one of the football players, holding his helmet and cleats, stopped to chat with us.

"Hey, there," he said, looking at me. "What are y'all up to?"

"Nothing much," I said, turning to pick up my bag.

"You're really good at those cheers," he said, ducking his head.

"Thanks. It's not that hard."

"You going for pizza?"

"We are," Jane said to him, stepping between him and me.

"I'll see you there," he said, but he didn't walk on. "Hey, Cal?"

"Yeah?"

"Do y'all still play touch football on your block?"

I laughed, "Not really. Why?"

"I just always thought that was so cool. You were a good quarterback."

"I was, wasn't I?"

Finally, he walked on ahead of us.

"He likes you," Jane said.

"Scott? I've known him since first grade."

"Well, I bet he asks you out."

"You mean so his mom can drive us to the movies or something? No, thanks."

"Still, if he asks you out, will you go?"

"I don't know. Do you think I should?"

She squeezed my hand, just for a second, and pulled me close enough to graze my cheek with her lips.

"I wouldn't if I were you," she whispered.

When we got to the pizza place, there were more than twenty kids there and some of the older guys had been drinking. The manager got upset with the crowd for being too loud and rowdy, and we had to leave before we could get our order. Jane managed to talk the waiter into giving her a pizza to go, and she grabbed me and pulled me out of the restaurant before anyone else saw us escape.

"Thanks," I said, taking a bite of the sausage pizza—my first ever—as we sat parked in front of my house. "It's so good!"

"This is decent," Jane said, "but someday I'll take you to my favorite Italian restaurant in LA. This doesn't even come close."

"Could we ever do that, really? Go anywhere, I mean. I've never even been on an airplane."

"If it's something we want to do bad enough, we'll find a way to make it happen."

"You are different, you know?"

"What do you mean…different?"

"You have big ideas. You don't let things stand in your way."

"I know what I want—usually. And I go after it. I've always been that way."

"I'm really glad we met. I feel so happy when I'm around you."

"You're very sweet. I almost wonder if you're too sweet."

"Too sweet for what?"

"This," she said, and she kissed me firmly on the lips, but only for a second. "You better get inside before—"

"Before what?"

"Just go. I'll see you soon."

I got out of the car and pushed the door shut, lingering a bit before turning to walk quickly to my door. I looked back and saw that she had waited to see me go inside before she drove off. I watched from the picture window in the front of our house, until she was out of sight. I touched my lips, which still tingled from the kiss, the memory of it playing over and over in my head. I couldn't believe it. A girl kissed me. And I had let it happen. I hadn't pushed her away or told her never to do that again. I wanted it. And I wanted it again. And though it seemed absurd that Jane and I could be together like that, the fantasy of it made me very happy.

CHAPTER TEN

My happiness faded the next morning when my mother, who had been in a progressively angrier mood since returning from her trip the week before, snapped at me about cleaning up my room. Even after I had spent all morning on it, she wouldn't let up.

"Look at this," she said, opening the closet door to reveal a jumble of clothes, shoes, a backpack, and several books. "You're a slob!" She stormed out of the room, stopping in the doorway to hiss over her shoulder, "Clean it up, Cal. I've had it."

Dejected, I spent another half hour folding and hanging and straightening and stacking. I looked over every inch of the room, searching for anything that was the least bit out of place. When Mom came back, she pointed at a flashlight sitting in the windowsill.

"Is that where that goes?"

"Mom! What's wrong?"

She looked at me intently and I felt uncomfortable. She let out a heavy sigh and closed her eyes. She hung her head and finally said, "I'm trying to sort some things out, Cal. I can't tell you what's going on. You wouldn't understand, and even if you did, it wouldn't be a good idea for you to know. I want you to trust me. Everything will be okay. I promise."

All I could do was nod. Then she pulled me close and gave me a hug. She squeezed me tightly and held on for so long, I started to get worried. On her way out she said, "And don't say anything to Rachel."

What would I say to Rachel? What was Mom up to? I was on edge all week and then Mom went out Friday night, telling me she'd be back late. I tried to stay up but fell asleep by eleven. Later I awoke to a banging on the door, like someone was trying to break it down. I looked at my digital clock in the dark. It was twelve thirty in the morning. I went to Mom's room but the bed was still made. I looked through the peephole in the front door and saw Dad standing on the porch. I really didn't want to, but I opened the door to the locked screen door since Mom would come in through the garage.

"Open it," he said.

"I don't think Mom would like that."

"Your mother's in trouble. Let me in."

I unlocked the screen and he opened it, pushing past me.

"What's going on?"

He ignored me and headed down the hall to her bedroom. I followed, knowing I should do something to stop him, but feeling helpless and scared.

"What are you doing?"

He ransacked her room, looking through all of her drawers until he found a pile of letters and other paper. "I'm sending someone to pick you up and take you to my apartment."

Then he left. I stood staring at the door for a while, confused and still scared. Did he say someone was coming for me? I couldn't think. What was going on? Where was my mother? I felt bad waking her, but I called Rachel.

"You can't come here," she said. "That's too obvious, but hey, I bet Jane would come and get you."

I ran to my room and threw a few things in a bag, enough for a day or two. Then I called Jane on her private phone line. "I'm sorry to call you so late."

Jane was groggy on the other end of the line. "It's okay. What's wrong? What do you need?"

"I need your help. Can you come and get me?"

"Now?"

"I know it's crazy. But something's going on with my mom. I don't know what. My dad is trying to take me away."

"I'll be there."

I was sitting on the curb waiting when Jane pulled up. I scrambled in and Jane took off like we were leaving the scene of a crime. I looked back as we made the turn at the end of the block. I saw a car pull into the driveway of our house.

"Somebody just went up to our house."

"Must be whoever your dad sent," Jane said. "Can you see who it is?"

It was too dark to make out a face, but I saw the car. "I can tell it's a Mustang."

By the time we got to Jane's, it was almost two a.m. We were too keyed up to fall asleep right away, so we went to the kitchen. Jane wanted to make me some special hot chocolate.

"This is going to take a little while," she said, pulling a package of dark chocolate out of the cabinet.

I sat on a barstool at the counter, watching, smiling, forgetting for the moment why I was there.

"My grandmother's recipe. You won't be disappointed."

When it was ready, she poured a cup and brought it to me, holding it in both hands. She put it to my lips.

"Don't worry. It won't burn your tongue."

I took a sip and Jane waited expectantly for my reaction. "Mmm, that's good."

"So," Jane said, running a finger along my forearm, "what the heck was going on there tonight?"

"It's so crazy. I can't make sense of it right now. My mom has been acting weird. And she told me there was something going on that she couldn't explain. But what my dad has to do with it, I have no idea."

"You know you can stay here as long as you need to." She brushed my hair back from my face.

"You're so nice to me."

"That's what friends do."

"What about your parents? Shouldn't you ask them?"

"They'll be fine."

"Hey, this could just be some crazy divorce drama between my mom and dad. It could all blow over by tomorrow." I didn't believe that, but I also didn't want Jane to think I was going to overstay my welcome.

"We can hope," Jane said, rinsing the cups and putting them into the dishwasher. She reached for my hand. "Come on. Let's get some sleep."

I watched her sleeping, unable to stop thinking about everything that had gone on over the past few days. My head throbbed with images of my dad's bizarre behavior. I'd never ever seen him like that. And what kind of trouble was my mother in? But even with all that running through my head, looking at Jane made my heart flutter. Even in her sleep, she held my hand. Hers was so soft.

I thought surely I had just fallen asleep when she woke me, nudging me to get up.

"Not yet," I said and pulled the covers over my head.

"Mom's making pancakes," Jane said. "You have to come down. Ted's already at the table."

"Tell them I'm sick."

"They're going to the airport in Amarillo in a little while," she said. "You can come back to bed when they leave."

I threw off the covers, frowning at Jane through eye slits.

"I didn't have to come get you last night—"

"Okay, okay," I said, moving toward the bathroom. "I'm coming."

I splashed water on my face, taking a hard look in the mirror. *Oh, god. I look like hell.* "Where's your makeup?"

"You don't need makeup," Jane said, appearing in the bathroom doorway. "Just brush your hair. I'll see you downstairs."

After working for several minutes to make myself presentable, I crept down the stairs. "What did you tell them?" I whispered to Jane.

"I said your electricity went out and your mom is away," Jane said in my ear.

I gave her the thumbs-up.

"Well, good morning," said Jane's mom, serving me a pile of pancakes with bacon. "I'm glad Jane could come to your rescue last night."

But the way she looked at me made me wonder how glad she really was. We sat at a high-top wooden table in the eating area of the kitchen where oversized French doors gave us a view of the patio and pool.

"I'm so happy to be here," I said. "Jane was a really good friend to come and get me. It was scary in the house with no electricity."

How easy it was to keep the lie going. I ate slowly, savoring every bite. I drifted off into a daydream about what it would be like to live in their house. I got so caught up in the dream that I didn't hear Mrs. Rawlings ask me how I liked my breakfast.

"Oh my gosh, the best ever," I said when she asked me again. "I can't thank you enough."

Jane's father came downstairs with two large, heavy-looking suitcases.

"We're about to head out," he said. "Jane, you're in charge. Don't let the house burn down."

"Dad, c'mon. You know me. I know how to take care of things."

"That's true," he said, turning to me. "Jane can hold down the fort better than any boy I've ever seen, including my son."

"Thanks a lot, Dad," Ted said as he came in from the outside.

"I can believe that," I said.

I smiled at Jane. Mrs. Rawlings caught my eye and gave me what Rachel and I would have called the hairy eyeball. I flinched.

"We're off," she said.

"I'll clean up," I said, jumping to take plates to the sink.

"Thank you, girls." She picked up her purse and keys. "Just so we know, are you staying over again tonight?"

Her tone was odd and I hesitated, looking at Jane.

"Uh—"

"We have to check on the electricity at her house," Jane said. "I'll let you know."

We watched them drive off in her dad's yellow Lincoln Town Car. "Your mom isn't happy about me being here."

"Just ignore that. She thinks Dad lets me get away with murder. She would have grounded me for taking the car out in the middle of the night."

"I can't believe you got away with that," Ted said. "Talk about the golden child."

"Give me a break," Jane said, throwing a dishtowel at him.

"Speaking of dads, I better leave mine a message about where I am so he doesn't worry. He'll be at work now."

"Don't you think he'll be mad that you disappeared?"

"Probably, but he'll get over it. This isn't about me. It's about my mom. Once he knows I'm safe, he won't think anything else about it."

Later, as we sat out on the patio, I started to feel antsy. I looked at my watch. "I'm going to call the house and see if my mom has made it back. When there was no answer, Jane suggested we drive by to see if we could tell anything from looking at the house. I agreed and we drove back to my neighborhood.

"Everything's the way I left it. She hasn't been back."

We walked across the street to Rachel's and rang the doorbell.

"Hey!" she said. "Your mom's still not back?"

"No. I haven't heard a word from her. But thank goodness for Jane."

"My idea, of course," Rachel said, smirking.

"And a good one," Jane agreed.

"I can't believe your dad came over like that," Rachel said. "Your mom would go crazy if she knew."

"I know. Don't say anything to anyone. But keep an eye on the house and if you see anything, call us right away."

We gave her Jane's private number.

"I'm on it," Rachel said, whispering and grasping the piece of paper with Jane's number.

"Don't be obvious," I said.

"Course not," Rachel said, straightening her back and folding her arms. "Don't worry."

As we drove back to Jane's, I suddenly was overcome by the jitters, like something really bad was about to happen or maybe had already happened. My breath came faster and I gripped the dashboard, trying to calm down.

"Are you okay?" Jane said.

"I think my mom has gotten herself into some serious trouble, but I don't know what it is."

"What do you think we should do?"

"We?"

"Of course."

"No, you don't need to get involved. If there is something dangerous going on, I don't want you near it."

"Well, that's not an option. You called me. Now I'm in it and you can't keep me out."

That night, I stayed at Jane's, with her parents' long-distance permission. I rode my bike to school, instead of getting a ride with Jane, because I didn't want to publicize my situation. After school, using Jane's bedroom as our base of operations, she and I started our mission to solve the mystery of Mom's disappearance.

Jane called the accountant's office where Mom worked and asked for her. She was told she hadn't come into work that day. The person answering said she didn't know when to expect her back in the office.

"My dad is really the only lead we have," I said. "He practically broke into the house, looking for something. And he found something. So he obviously knows something, but he's not going to tell me anything. Maybe we shouldn't even be trying to do this. We're in over our heads."

"Why so negative?" Jane said. "We just need some inspiration. Let's go for a swim."

She lent me one of her suits and we dressed in the poolhouse. The deck furniture was all piled together on one end of the pool like it had just been cleaned. It was made of some fancy wood. You could tell by looking at it that it was heavy. She went over to get two of the chaises for us. They were on rollers.

"Let me help," I said.

"It's okay. I got it."

When she picked up the end of the heavy chaise, her biceps flexed and the definition in her shoulders showed. Before I could stop myself, this weird sound came out of me, sort of a groan and a sigh. I slapped my hand to my mouth.

"Did you say something?" Jane asked.

"Oh, no, nothing. I just…Your muscles are so…nice. How do you do that?"

"We have a weight room. I'll show you later. You could look like this too."

"You have a weight room?"

"They set it up for Ted, really. My mother's not crazy about me using it. She doesn't believe in muscles. For girls." She twirled around like a ballerina and curtsied.

I laughed and helped her set up the towels on the lounges. She stood up for a stretch, arching her back and raising her arms over her head. She pulled her hair back and twisted it into a ponytail. Was she taunting me in that skimpy suit? My heart sped up. My mouth got dry. The throbbing between my legs…

"What if we were to spy on your dad?" she said, sitting next to me.

"What?" I couldn't remember what we were talking about.

"If he knows what's going on, maybe we can figure it out by following him."

"I don't know—"

"Do you have a key to his apartment?"

"I know where he keeps one in case he gets locked out, but—"

"And you know his work schedule…"

"It feels weird to spy on him."

"Then why not just talk to him?"

"That's barking up the wrong tree. He won't take me seriously."

"Okay, well…Do you have another idea?"

Jane sighed in exasperation, staring into the pool. After a few seconds of silence, I gave in.

"You're right. What else can we do? We have to go check out his apartment. See what we can find."

"Now you're talking," Jane said. "When do we go?"

"He's working a day shift tomorrow so we could go after school."

"Okay, that's settled. Now, let's have some fun."

She pulled me off the chaise and shoved me into the deep end of the pool. We came to the surface at the same time and she pulled me to her. We floated on our backs, holding hands. When we got to the shallow end, she got behind me, wrapped her arms around me. I closed my eyes."

"What are you thinking?" she said.

"I can't tell you."

"Why not?"

"I'm too scared."

She turned me around and examined my face, touching my lips with her finger.

"Don't be scared. I'll take care of you."

"I don't mean about my mom."

"I know," she said.

She put her arms around me and whispered into my ear, "You can trust me."

We heard tires on gravel. It was Rachel. Her mom was dropping her off. My heart sank as Jane and I pushed away from each other, my hope for another kiss fading with the sound of Rachel's voice hollering hello.

CHAPTER ELEVEN

After school the next day, Jane and I headed to my dad's apartment. Rachel had a math tutor she couldn't dodge. Jane parked her mother's car at the edge of the parking lot. It was a two-story garden-style building with a pool in the center. I hadn't been very social when visiting my dad there, so I didn't think anyone really knew who I was, but I had disguised myself just to be on the safe side.

"You look ridiculous," Jane said, laughing as I got out of the car wearing a jumpsuit, heels, a big floppy hat, and sunglasses. I didn't look anything like myself.

"Don't laugh! We have to be serious to pull this off." I lifted my sunglasses and gave her a look.

His apartment was on the second floor. We walked upstairs and down the breezeway to his unit. I pulled a key box out from under the windowsill. The key was inside.

"Here we go," I said.

"Let's do it."

It was a small apartment. Two small bedrooms, a bathroom, a living room and a kitchen.

"Where should we look? What are we looking for?" I said.

"Evidence," Jane said. "Note, receipts, maps, recordings…"

"Recordings?"

"Maybe there's an answering machine with messages. We don't know what he's been up to."

"Oh, yeah. He has one of those because of his job at the plant. I'll check his desk."

"Okay, I'm going through the trash."

A few minutes later, I found something in the bedroom. "Oh, man, I can't believe this."

Jane ran into the bedroom. "What?"

"This is what he stole from her dresser the other night." I held up a fistful of letters. "Love letters."

Jane started reading through the letters. "Wow," she said. "I wonder who this guy is."

I didn't want to read them.

"What's his name?"

"He signs the letters 'Hank.'"

I leaned against the doorjamb, beginning to regret this whole thing.

"This is just the beginning," Jane said. "Your dad only swiped these a few days ago. There's got to be more."

"The message machine is over here on the counter."

We rewound it to the beginning. Most of the messages were routine, including my message about being at Jane's, but we heard one that was different. It was from a woman named Marcie. The message was date-stamped from the night Dad had burst into Mom's house.

"Tom," the message said. "You won't believe what I just heard about your ex. She's playin' with fire. Call me."

I slid all the way to the floor, groaning.

"What does that mean?"

"I don't know, but whatever it is she's talking about, is what we need to know."

We headed back to Jane's by way of my house.

"I don't know why I keep thinking we're going to pull up and she's going to be there on the porch, mad as a hornet," I said. I teared up just a little as we drove by my house.

"Hey, there!" Rachel called out from her stoop.

We stopped the car and rolled down the window.

"Can I come along with y'all?"

"Come on," Jane said, unlocking the back door.

"There's a car that's been cruisin' by every so often," Rachel said.

"What kind of car?" I asked.

"A nice one, kinda long with a landau roof. It's a dark green color. Maybe a Cadillac."

"Who was driving?"

"I couldn't see. The windows were tinted really dark."

"How many time did you see it? All weekend?"

"Yeah," Rachel said. "Once or twice a day."

"What do you think that's about?"

"Maybe they're looking for you," Rachel said.

"Who? That gives me the creeps," I said. "Let's get out of here."

Back at Jane's we struggled about what to do next.

"Who is Marcie?" Jane asked.

"I've been wracking my brain. I think she's this woman who's been trying to date my dad."

"I know her," said Rachel. "She's that short blonde who sits in the front row of the choir, right in the middle."

"Any idea how to find her?" Jane asked.

"Church," Rachel and I said at the same time.

"It's choir practice tonight," Rachel said. "Think she'd be there?"

"There's a good chance," I said. "Let's check it out."

We decided to wait in the church parking lot, hoping to spot Marcie. Rachel hopped out and snaked her way through the cars, keeping her head down, so she could watch everyone as they came out of the door.

It was dark when people started to emerge from the church to go home. A petite blonde crossed in front of us, and I grabbed Jane's arm and whispered, "That's her."

Rachel jumped back in the car just as Marcie got into her Ford Mustang and pulled out of the parking lot.

"Don't get too close," I said.

"Don't worry."

"Hey, I think that's the same car I saw pull into our driveway Friday night after you picked me up."

We followed her, and before long, we realized we were headed into Dad's apartment complex.

"This is interesting," Jane said.

"Let's park around the other side," I said. "There's a back staircase."

I took them up the service stairs and to the back of his apartment. There was an unlocked storage closet on the back of his unit.

"We can hear what they're saying," I said, pointing to a dryer vent in the closet. "And you can see the kitchen through this crack."

He invited her in and offered her iced tea. He poured them both a glass and they sat down on stools at the counter. She touched his arm gently.

"How'er you holdin' up, honey?" she asked, a little too syrupy, I thought.

"I'm fine," he said, waving off her concern.

"You look tired," she said. "Did you get any sleep last night?"

"I can't sleep. Cal doesn't want to have anything to do with me. My wife is missing."

"She's not your wife, honey," Marcie said. "Do you mind if I smoke?"

He grabbed an ashtray from the cabinet and pushed it in front of her.

"What did you find out when you went through her things?" Marcie asked, digging in her purse for her cigarettes and lighter.

"I could see she's got something going on with him. He's sweet talking her. But the other stuff—"

"Look, Tom. If what I heard is true, you need to give up on her. You don't want to get anywhere near all that."

He squirmed in his seat. "I'm telling you, I can talk sense into her. She'll listen to me. Now, where is she?"

"I don't know."

"Can you find out?"

"The boys I know are in the dark. They don't know where she disappeared to the other night," she said, taking a gulp of the iced tea. "And Hank is playing dumb, like he can't control her."

"You told me you would help me get her back," he said, more agitated. "I never would have spied on her that way if you hadn't said it would help me understand what's going on."

"I know, honey. I know. But it's looking like she gave everybody the slip."

"What? You think she's in on whatever this is?"

"It's just...Tom...There's more to this than we thought."

"She was a bored housewife. She got tricked into an affair by the big man in town who could buy her things and take her places."

I could see his lips were tight. I thought he might cry.

"Oh, I think there's a lot more going on here than that, Tom."

"What do you know about it?"

"Well," Marcie said, taking a long drag on her cigarette. "I know she played you. And she's playin' you still."

Dad stood up and punched the wall, knocking a hole into the drywall next to the kitchen cabinets. All three of us gasped. He looked over in our direction.

"Did you hear something?"

"Just you, acting like a heathen about that woman."

"Look," he said, "I know how you feel about Joyce. But I'm not ready to give up on her just yet. So I'm asking you one last time. How can I find out what's happened to her?"

Marcie looked at the floor and shook her head.

"I can't get a straight answer out of the boys. They're nervous as hell. The only thing I've been able to pick up on, and it's not much, is that there's something about Palo Duro Canyon."

CHAPTER TWELVE

I was trembling as we drove back to Jane's. "I've got to find her," I said, staring straight ahead, my hands gripping the dashboard.

Rachel and Jane didn't say anything the whole way back. It was as if they were stunned into a trance by what they'd heard. Once we got back to Jane's, I did my best to focus on what to do next and not dwell on what might or might not have happened.

"This is a bigger deal than we thought, Jane. Are you okay with us using your room as our headquarters?"

"Of course," Jane said as she led the way. "Let's get started."

It was Friday and the football team had a bye week, so we could get right to work. We organized Jane's bedroom into our war room. We borrowed a flip chart from Jane's dad's office down the hall, along with a box of index cards, legal pads, and pencils. We found a map of the Texas panhandle and put that on the wall. The telephone sat in the middle of the table, looking like a hotline.

"What should we do now?" Rachel asked.

"We put one foot in front of the other until we figure something out," I said. "We can't forget what we heard in the shed. Take some notes."

Rachel grabbed a legal pad and a pen. I paced around the room.

"Ready," she said, crouched over the desk, ready to take dictation.

"My dad said something about this guy Hank being a big man around town. We need to find out who this guy is."

"Who is Hank?" Rachel said as she wrote in bold letters on the legal pad.

"Your mom's having an affair and then she disappears. Then the guy she's having the affair with claims he doesn't know where she is. It doesn't add up. He's lying," Jane said.

"Hank is lying," Rachel said, printing it on the page.

"I agree," I said. "Either she went with him willingly or he kidnapped her. But he has to be involved."

"We're back to the first question," Rachel said. "Who is Hank?"

Just then, Ted came into the room carrying a few letters.

"The mail from your house," he said, tossing the letters and my keys onto the table, catching his breath from the bike ride over.

"Thanks for doing that, Ted. I just couldn't go near there after I heard about that creepy car prowling around."

"I gotta go," he said. "Good luck, y'all."

"Hey!" Rachel said. "Don't forget what Marcie said at the end."

"Oh, yeah," Jane said, "something about a canyon."

"Palo Duro Canyon," Rachel said.

I got up and pointed to the map. "It's here. It's a state park. We used to go there for hiking and exploring, looking for arrowheads when we were kids. It's about an hour and a half from here. But I don't understand what it could have to do with anything."

"Hey, y'all," Rachel said, holding up one of the pieces of mail Ted had brought over from my house. "This looks like it might be something important."

It was a flat, brown envelope addressed to me in a dark marker. Carrie Ann Long, with my address.

"Carrie Ann," said Jane. "So that's your name."

"Don't call me that!"

"Go on. Open it," Jane said.

"There aren't any stamps on it. Someone just put it in the box," I said.

Inside was an 8.5x11 photograph. It must have been taken at dusk, so it was hard to make out everything in the picture. Jane brought a magnifying glass out of a drawer in the desk.

"Look," she said, pointing to a posted sign that showed up in the background behind some rocks and bushes.

The sign read *Hackberry Camp Area*.

"Hackberry," I said. "Is that the name of the camp we used to go to in Girl Scouts?"

"The one in Palo Duro Canyon!" Rachel said.

"What does this mean? Who would have sent it to you?"

"I have no idea. We need a map of the canyon. I want to see exactly where this camp is."

"You know what? My dad has lots of maps in his desk," Jane said. "I bet you anything he's got state park maps in his office."

All three of us went down the hall to Mr. Rawlings' office. There were lots of maps hanging on the walls showing salt caverns and referencing petroleum reserves. I noticed a picture of Jane's dad with President Nixon.

"Jane, your dad knows him?"

Jane looked at the picture. She turned up her nose at the thought. "Oh, that was when my dad was getting an award for something about oil and national security. It's not like they're friends or anything."

"Forget about that, y'all. Here's the maps of the canyon," Rachel said, pulling some out of a drawer.

"Here's Hackberry," I said. "It looks like this site is the biggest one in the canyon."

"I think we have to check it out, don't you?" Jane asked.

"It's the only clue we've got," I said.

"Let's go camping," Rachel said. "We have camping equipment in our garage."

"Okay, girls, it's getting late, but we need to get going so we'll have the whole weekend," Jane said.

"Wow," I said, looking at my watch. "I had no idea it was this late."

"I'm going to my room to get my stuff." Rachel smiled. "Hey, Jane, how do you like that. I've got my own room in your house!"

"I love it," Jane said. "I always wanted a sister."

After Rachel left the room, Jane pulled me over to the loveseat near the window where we sat side by side.

"I can't imagine how you're feeling right now," she said, playing with my hair.

"I feel numb," I said. "Like I stumbled into someone else's dream. Or nightmare…"

She put her arm around me and I rested my head on her shoulder.

"I wish I could stay here like this. Maybe forever," I said.

"I wish we could, too, but we've got work to do."

We rushed back to Caroline Street where Rachel rode up and down the block on her bike, scouting for any trouble, while Jane and I quickly got the tent and other camping gear out of the garage and into the car.

"What's going on here?"

It was Rachel's dad. We thought no one was home.

"Uh," I said, "we…I mean…we thought…"

"Hey!" Rachel screeched into the garage on her bike. "Dad, remember when I told you about the origami butterflies and how they like certain kinds of bushes that are hard to find?"

"Yes, but I thought you were just spinning one of your yarns."

"Well, we are going on a hunt for those bushes."

Jane and I looked back and forth between Rachel and her dad.

"What kind of hunt?"

"We're gonna camp out at Jane's. You know, on their property. So we can scout out the landscape in search of the butterfly bush."

Rachel's dad scratched his head and looked at Rachel as if trying to decipher her for the millionth time. Then he looked at me and Jane.

"Everyone understand that I expect you to look out for each other?"

We all nodded and quickly jumped into the car and took off. Since we weren't sure exactly what we were getting into, we shopped for enough food and water to last for several days.

"What if we end up missing school?" Rachel asked.

"We'll cross that bridge if we come to it," I said. "Let's not worry about it for now."

"We should make it into the park just before the gate closes," I said. "That's eight o'clock."

"I've been looking at the map and I think maybe we want to camp at the Sagebrush site," Jane said. "It seems like the best location."

"That's here," Rachel said. "Looks like it's not far from Hackberry."

Just after six p.m. we pulled out of town, headed toward Palo Duro Canyon. None of us said anything for a while, like we were caught up in our own thoughts.

"Do y'all want a Coke?" Rachel asked eventually, pulling one out of the cooler.

"No, thanks," Jane said.

"I'd split one with you," I said, looking over my shoulder into the backseat where Rachel was shoehorned in among all the gear and supplies.

"This could be a trap, you know," Jane said, squinting into the sun as it dropped down over the plains ahead.

"I've been thinking about that," I said.

"I just got goose bumps," Rachel said, shaking it off.

"We have to hope whoever sent that envelope was a good guy." Jane gripped the steering wheel a little tighter.

"And keep our wits about us," I said, glancing at the other two.

Just then, we heard a huge bang that sounded like an explosion and the car leaned toward the front passenger side and bumped hard against the pavement. We all screamed at the same time.

"What was that!"

"Oh, God," Jane said, slowing down and pulling off to the side of the road. "I think it's a blowout."

"The tire?" Rachel asked from the floor in the back, where she'd been thrown when the car careened to the right.

"What do we do now?" I got out and looked at the ripped rubber.

"Well, we have to get the spare on," Jane said with a grimace.

"Do you know how to do that?" Rachel asked.

"I do," Jane said, "but it's not easy and I've never done it without my dad or my brother."

We had to empty all our stuff out of the trunk to get the spare tire. Jane put the jack together and placed it on the bumper. She started to pump the lever, lifting the car up off the ground. I couldn't take my eyes off her as the sweat gleamed on her muscles and poured in rivulets off her shoulder. Rachel gave me a shove.

"We should be doing something," she said.

"Should we pull the old tire off?" I asked.

A truck full of teenage boys drove by us and slowed down.

"Hey, y'all need some help?" They grinned at us.

"Maybe," Rachel answered, grinning back.

"I think we're okay," Jane said, "but thanks."

"C'mon, Jane, would it hurt?"

"We have to stay focused, Rachel," I said, waving the boys on.

She let out an exasperated sigh. "I don't know how much I like having a girl who can do all this. It's like we don't even need boys anymore."

We left the trashed tire on the side of the road and took off with the spare in place.

"We'll have to get this fixed eventually," Jane said, "but it will get us there tonight."

We were behind schedule, but by seven-fifty, we were pulling off Texas State Highway 217 and up to the canyon's main gate. We paid the fifty cents to get in plus another two-fifty for the campsite. The gatekeeper was a chunky woman with rough reddish cheeks and stringy gray-blond hair. Her khaki-colored park ranger uniform looked two sizes too small. She smiled at us as she taped our ticket to the windshield.

"Y'all be careful in there. There's been some coyotes runnin' round the last few months. It's been dry, 'course, so they're lookin' for food."

"We'll watch out," Rachel piped in from the backseat.

We drove on the cracked concrete road past the rim cabins and the visitor center. The Sagebrush Camp was across from the Pioneer Amphitheater.

"That's where they do *Texas*," Rachel said.

"What's that?" Jane asked.

"It's a musical. Kinda like Broadway," Rachel said.

"I don't think it's as good as Broadway," I said.

"Well, anyway, it's really great."

As we pulled into the camping area, the road turned to red dirt. It was dark by then and we left the headlights on as we unpacked the car and set up camp. There were only a few other campers there, so we had our pick of sites.

Rachel and I did most of the setup while Jane found some firewood. I was grateful to have so much work to do. It kept me from thinking too deeply about what all of this really meant. I had a thousand questions in my head about what my mother could be involved in, and whenever it was quiet, the questions would hit me like I was a punching bag. So it was better if I worked myself to exhaustion.

We laid out a tarp on the ground, then set up the three-person tent, struggling to drive the stakes into the hard, dry clay. We turned on all of our camp lanterns and flashlights so we could shut off the headlights. It got chilly in the canyon at night, so we wanted to get a fire going in the firepit. Jane took the ax and split some of the logs. Rachel gave me the hairy eyeball when Jane stripped down to a T-shirt so she wouldn't catch anything with the ax. But I couldn't help it. I had to stare as her muscles flexed in the lantern light when she swung that ax over her head and split a log with one stroke.

"Nice arms, Jane," Rachel said, glancing at me when she said it.

"Thanks for noticing," Jane said, smirking back at her.

"You're like a puppy," Rachel whispered to me.

"Whatever," I whispered back.

We were all hungry by then, so we decided to eat something before looking around any further. We had boiled some hot dogs, stuffed them in buns and wrapped them in foil. We heated them up on the fire.

"Not bad," said Jane, pouring on the mustard.

"How about s'mores," Rachel said, taking a Hershey bar and some marshmallows out of a bag. "Where are the graham crackers?"

"Over there," I said.

"This is pretty nice," Jane said, looking up at the clear sky full of stars.

"Did you hear that?" I said as I raised my hand toward the brush where I thought I heard something.

We got quiet, listening.

"I don't hear anything," Rachel said.

"I'm a little jumpy," I said.

"Let's take a look around," Jane suggested.

We put on our jackets and took flashlights with us as we inspected the arca right around the site. We walked back out to the main road, passing a few tents on our way.

Suddenly, Rachel grabbed both of us and whispered, "Look out!"

In the beam of her flashlight was a coyote.

"Be still," I said.

We stood like statues until the animal trotted off, ignoring us. Then we headed past the Trading Post and the Old West Stables and eventually came to the entrance to the Hackberry

Camp. It had much larger sites and there were several big RVs parked and running their generators. We walked around the camp, saying hello to folks who were sitting outside enjoying the evening.

"All seems pretty normal," Rachel said.

"Yeah," I said. "Nothing suspicious yet."

"Back to our camp?" Jane said.

When we got back to the tent, we were all exhausted.

"I am worn out," Rachel said. "I haven't had this much brain work since geometry."

"Yeah, I'm beat," I said.

"Me too," Jane said. "I'm turning in."

We pulled the sleeping bags out of the car and made sure all the food was in the trunk, away from prying paws. I'm pretty sure we all fell asleep the minute we laid down.

CHAPTER THIRTEEN

The next morning we showered in the camp restrooms, ate breakfast, and planned out the day. We decided we would go back to Hackberry Camp and look at it in the daylight. If we didn't find anything, we'd spend the rest of the day hiking and head back to town.

"What are we looking for, anyway?" Rachel asked.

"I have to believe there was a good reason why someone sent me that picture of Hackberry," I said. "If this guy Hank is involved in whatever this is, someone at that camp may know him."

"True," Jane said. "We should interview people."

"Interview?" Rachel said.

"You know, just ask them if they've seen anything suspicious. If they've noticed anything strange or out of place."

Rachel nodded. "Okay. I got it."

When we got back over to Hackberry, we split up. I struck up a conversation with a family that turned out to be from Colorado. They were a couple with two little kids. They had only been at the camp for a day or two and didn't have much to say about anything they'd seen. I kept moving and found a man, probably in his forties, wearing jeans and cowboy boots. He was working on his truck.

"Hi," I said, waving as I walked up.

He looked at me but didn't say anything.

"Just wondering if you know much about the canyon."

He gave me a look like I was bothering him. "I been around."

"Have you ever met a guy named Hank?"

He put his tools down and turned toward me. "No," he said, "and I don't think you want to either."

"But you know who he is?"

"Let's just say I know enough to know where I shouldn't stick my nose." He turned back to his truck. I stayed put, thinking he might have more to say. He looked back at me again. "You still here?"

"I just thought, if you know him, or something about him, maybe you could tell me."

"Look, what's your name?"

"Cal."

"Look, Cal, you need to stay away from that guy."

"But who is he?"

"His last name is Hart. He's into some very shady stuff. Criminal stuff. It's about oil and gas. That's all I know."

"Really?"

"Now, go on. Get out of this canyon."

I walked away feeling anxious and a little panicky. My mother was involved in something way over her head as far as I could tell, and I had no idea how I was going to help her out of it. I looked up and saw Jane, coming from the other side of the camp, almost running toward me, her eyes bright with excitement.

"What did you find?"

"That couple over there," she said, pointing to a big RV with Illinois plates, "said they saw something strange here about a week ago."

"Okay, sounds promising."

"It was late one night. After midnight. An RV pulled in here and a little while later another big truck pulled in beside it. They sat there idling their engines for a couple of hours and then the truck left. About an hour after that, the RV left."

"Interesting."

"It was all over and done by four a.m., well before daylight," Jane said. "What could you be doing out here in the middle of the night, except something you shouldn't be doing?"

"Were there any markings or names on the truck or the RV?"

"Nothing they could see in the dark."

Just then, Rachel rode up on a horse—a big gray mare.

"What the heck are you doing?" I said.

"The people I talked to were horse people and I told them I love to ride, so they offered me Bessie here," she said, giving the horse a love pat. "And don't worry. I got some info, too," she said, sticking her tongue out at me.

"Okay, but get down off that horse. I don't like having to look up at you like this," I said.

She slid off the saddle and jumped to the ground. "They said they come out here from Amarillo almost every weekend this time of year. They've noticed that once in a while on Saturday night, there's a lot of truck noise coming from somewhere way out in the canyon. Sometimes it goes from midnight until before sunrise."

"Sounds like what Jane heard."

"These folks complained to the rangers, but they say the trucks have a permit for whatever it is they're doing."

"Let's find out who got the permit," Jane said.

"We need to be extra careful," I said. "I talked to a guy who said Hank—his last name is Hart—is some kind of criminal mastermind. Oil and gas. If Hart is the one behind all this middle of the night stuff, we need to watch it. We're getting in deep."

Rachel returned the horse to her owners and we all headed back to the tent. We were just sitting down to talk about what to do next when the woman who had been at the guard station when we first came in drove up in her pickup.

"Just checkin' on you gals," she said. "Everything okay over here?"

"Actually," I said, "we were wondering about something."

The woman threw her truck into park and got out. "Okeydokey," she said. "What can I do ya for?"

"If someone gets a permit to do something here in the canyon, is there a way to find out who they are?"

The woman looked at me like she wasn't sure she wanted to answer me. "Well, yes, in theory."

"What does that mean?" Rachel asked.

"Well, this is a state park and permits are public information. It's just that the records aren't always…real nice and neat."

"Would you mind if we took a look?" I asked.

"What exactly are you looking for?"

I told her what we'd heard from the folks in the camp.

"Well, it's true they have a permit and it would be on their vehicles. Are you wanting to know who they are?"

"That's right," I said.

"Why do you need to know, if I can ask?"

"It's for a school project," Rachel said. "We have to research how the state processes permits, how they decide to say yes or no."

"Well, I don't know their names, but you're welcome to come over to HQ and look through the permit applications. That's where you'd find it, if it's there, but I wouldn't get my hopes up."

"Could we go now?" I asked.

"I can ride you up there now, if you want. You'll have to walk back."

We all jumped into the pickup, Rachel riding in the bed.

"Nice job," I whispered to Rachel, who gave me a thumbs-up.

"My name's Missy, by the way," she said to me and Jane, who squeezed in next to her.

When we got to HQ, Missy showed us into the file room, which was dark and dank and smelled of molding paper.

"Gross!" Rachel choked through the dust that rained down on her as she pulled a manila folder off the top of a tall metal filing cabinet.

We must have been at it for two hours when Jane found something. "Look. This is a permit application for tanker truck storage. It says it was approved last year."

"Who applied for it?" I asked.

"It says Brazos River, Incorporated. It's signed by—oh my god! By Hank Hart!"

"Whoa," Rachel said. "Pay dirt."

"What the heck are they doing with those tankers? It's not just storage if they're running the engines all night," I said as we made our way back to camp.

"Yeah. They may have a permit, but it's not for what they're doing. If the guy you met is right, whatever it is, it's probably illegal," Jane said, "but how are they getting away with it?"

"This is a little scary," Rachel said.

"Let's just take the night off and start over in the morning," I said. "Maybe we'll wake up with a brilliant idea."

But before we got a chance to get back to our camp, a woman wearing a khaki-colored western-style uniform, stopped us.

"Girls," she said. "Hold on. My name is Officer Gillette. I'm a Texas Ranger and I'd like to have a word with you."

We stopped in our tracks, looking at each other like we'd been caught shoplifting. I stared at the gun on her hip and the cowboy-style hat on her head.

"What did we do, Officer?" Rachel asked.

"Nothing. It's not that. I just want to ask you a few questions. Let's go over to those benches and have a seat."

What choice did we have? We followed her to the picnic benches and sat in a row on the same side of the table facing her. She looked to be in her late twenties. She took out a notepad and a pen.

"First let me have your names, addresses, and ages."

We gave her the information and she hesitated when I said mine, making what seemed like extra notes next to my name. Then she continued.

"Missy in the guardhouse said you girls have been poking around in the headquarters office, looking for permits. Could you tell me why?"

I cleared my throat and sat up as straight as I could. "We are investigating my mother's disappearance," I said, mustering all the sternness I could.

Officer Gillette stayed silent for a few seconds, like she was sizing me up. A drop of sweat slid down my back and into my underwear.

"I see," she said. "But you must have reported this to the police?"

"No," I said. "I'm not sure she isn't just off on a trip somewhere. So I didn't want to bother the police just yet. I figured I might find her on my own."

"I'm not sure that's a good idea," Officer Gillette said, closing her notebook. "You should leave this kind of thing to the authorities. And you should get back home."

"We have clues," Rachel said insistently as the officer stood. "We've interviewed people. We know some things. Like there's this guy Hank Hart who's supposed to be a bad guy. And he has a permit for tankers in the canyon and we think he's up to something. And we think Cal's mom knows this guy. So we're worried about her."

She paused and sat back down. She spoke in a hushed tone, almost a whisper. "Okay, girls. I'm going to tell you as much as I can, but you have to promise me that you will leave this canyon and get back home first thing tomorrow."

We nodded in unison, our eyes wide, waiting like three chicks in a nest, waiting to be fed.

"Hank Hart is a very bad man. He runs an organized crime ring. And your mother is involved with him."

I gasped. Rachel and Jane both grabbed for my hand.

"They're having an affair," she said, glancing sheepishly at me. "We don't know whether she's part of the criminal operation or not."

"I don't believe Joyce could ever do something like that," Rachel said. "They must have kidnapped her."

"I'm sure that's it," Jane said.

"Why would you even think she could be a part of it?" I asked, my voice cracking.

"The truth is, we just don't know. The investigation is ramping up. We think they're about to make a big move. We have a team meeting at the courthouse in Amarillo tomorrow. I may know more after that. I'll stay in touch with you and update you as much as I can."

As she left, she took a card out of her pocket and handed it to me.

"Call me if you need anything. If you see or hear anything."

I looked at the card. *Beverly Gillette, Staff Lt.*

"Okay, L..lew..tenant?" I said.

"Just call me Bev."

She took off and the park ranger gave us a bumpy ride back to camp. As the sun began to drop and a chill filled the air, we built a fire and tried to relax. I stared into the fire, rocking back and forth with my arms tightly around my knees. I had the weirdest feeling, like maybe this was all a dream and I would wake up any minute with my mom yelling at me to clean up my room.

Rachel broke the silence. "You know what we have to do, don't you?"

"What?" I asked.

"We have to get into that team meeting."

"We're not getting into that meeting," I said.

"I don't mean get in really. I mean listen in somehow. Sneaky like."

"Rachel's right," Jane said.

"Are you two crazy? There's no way. If we got caught, we would be expelled from school or worse."

"You just have to know how to play this," Jane said.

"Do tell."

"First of all, we can do it without getting caught. But even if we do get caught, we play up the mom/daughter thing. All we're trying to do is reunite a mother and her daughter."

"Even if I agreed with you, I couldn't let you two risk it. I'll go. But I'm going alone."

"Look, Cal," Rachel said, taking me by the shoulders. "You and I have been friends since birth. This is the worst thing that's ever happened to either one of us and we're sticking together until the end."

The next morning we got up early and drove into Amarillo. Bev had said the meeting was going to be at the courthouse, so we stopped at a phone booth to look up the address. It was on East Fifth Street. It was Sunday, so the building was closed for regular business and the parking lot was wide open, except for a few Ranger patrol cars parked up near the front entrance. We pulled in slowly and parked in a corner away from the building. We didn't see anyone.

"Let's go to the back of the building and see if there's a way in," I said.

"Act normal," Rachel said as we strolled slowly through the parking lot. "In case somebody drives by."

The streets were quiet like a ghost town. We got to the back of the building without crossing paths with another human being.

"Let's take a look over there," Jane said, pointing to the large trash bins that hulked close to the edge of one corner of the building.

When we got closer, we saw an oversized metal door, big enough to drive a truck through, propped open with a brick. We crept to it, peering into the four-inch opening to find a dark corridor. Jane tried opening the door, but needed our help because of the weight of it. Once we were inside, we stood still, waiting for our eyes to adjust to the darkness. A sliver of light shone from under a door at the far end of the corridor, just enough that we could see where to walk.

We held our breath as we tried the door. It opened! We were in the basement of the courthouse with no idea where to go next. We found the elevators, but of course it was too risky to take them.

"Over here," I said, noticing a set of swinging doors that led to a stairway.

The stairs were wide and made of marble. The same swinging doors guarded the main corridor of each floor as we progressed upward. It was eerily quiet on the first floor as we listened at the doors, and the same on the third floor. But when we reached the fourth, we heard voices and the sound of chairs pushing across the floor as people settled into what we knew had to be the meeting.

The three of us exchanged glances, Rachel's eyes wide with what I felt sure were second thoughts and Jane's confident and encouraging. I lifted my finger to my lips and turned to push the door open just enough to see into the hallway. I caught a glimpse of someone pulling the doors shut on what must have been the meeting room. I turned to the other two.

"That's got to be it," I said. "But I'm not sure how we're going to hear what's going on in there."

"Look," Jane said, "the restroom is right next to it. Maybe there's a vent or something we can listen through."

We pushed the stairway door open, took a quick look around, and dashed as quickly and quietly as we could straight to the restroom. Hoping we didn't get surprised by anyone inside, we just stepped on in. We were lucky. It was all clear.

"That's what we're looking for," I said, pointing to a grate on the wall just below the crease of the ceiling.

The sinks were on the same wall and above the sinks was a stone ledge that extended six or eight inches from the wall, enough for a purse or a makeup bag. A mirror covered most of the wall.

"If I stand on the ledge, I can reach the grate, but you two will have to boost me up if I'm going to get inside. And then I have to hope I can hear them."

We stood on the sinks, and then I stepped onto the ledge. I was able to reach the grate and pull it down, revealing a generous passage into the ceiling. Jane and Rachel braced themselves against the wall and offered their gripped hands as a stirrup for each of my feet. I climbed in, we counted to three, and they boosted me up. I slipped at first, but grabbed a metal brace that I used to haul myself into the duct. I was in.

I crawled along the dusty surface, listening as hard as I could. After a few feet, I saw another grate, and sure enough, it was on the wall of the meeting room. I could hear them loud and clear. And I could even see, though my view was limited by the hatched metal of the grate. A man in a dark suit stood at the end of a long table. The room was filled with men, maybe ten or twelve, and Officer Gillette.

"Let's get started," said the standing man, introducing himself as Colonel Matt Jones. He pulled a screen down from the ceiling and turned the lights low. "Go ahead," he indicated to one of the other men. A projector lit up the screen, showing photographs of several men. "This is the Brazos River Gang, the main members being from the same family," he said. "They run various criminal enterprises in the Southwest and Mexico. Some weapons, some prostitution, some financial scams."

Brazos River Gang.

"No drugs. They seem to have some scruples over that," Colonel Jones said.

"This first guy you see is Hank Hart," said Bev. "The other three are his sons, Will, Warren, and Clay."

That's him. I've seen that man with my mother.

"Warren's the smart one. Will is not the sharpest tool in the shed, and Clay is somewhat the reluctant partner, but he likes the money," said Bev. "But all three boys have one thing in common. They're ruthless and they don't mind spilling blood if necessary."

I felt the blood drain from my head and thought I might faint. The projector flipped over to a slide showing oil derricks and tanker trucks.

Colonel Jones continued, "We all know the price of gas has gone through the roof since the Organization of Petroleum Exporting Countries, they call it OPEC, started an oil embargo early this year. They're not selling us the oil, which means we don't have enough supply for our cars here in this country. Long lines at the pump. People fighting over gasoline and stealing it if they can. We think this gang is stealing gasoline and reselling it cheap for a huge profit to themselves."

"How do they get away with it?" asked someone in the room.

"They have upstream and downstream partners. Everyone's making so much money, they're willing to protect the operation," Bev said.

"They're tapping small enough amounts from any given source that it hasn't been enough for anyone to notice," said Colonel Jones. "We think they're working with lower level employees at the oil refineries. Then they're paying off minor players along the way."

"They appear to be masking a tanker as an RV," said Bev. "They offload the payload to smaller trucks that disburse to various locations where they sell to retail outlets. All along the way participants take a cut."

I think that's what's going on in the canyon.

Bev asked if the colonel thought they should give an update on what they knew about my mom.

"Joyce Long," he said. "She started seeing Hart about a year and a half ago."

What? I couldn't believe it. My mother had been seeing someone behind my father's back for that long?

"This guy Hart always has a woman on the side. Joyce happens to be that one right now."

I dropped my head into my hands. This was too much.

"She's lasted longer than most and we're working on a theory that she may be causing some dissent among the troops. Some of the guys are starting to question Hart's focus. They think maybe she's become too important to him. They don't like the idea of him being the least bit distracted."

"Are we concerned about her safety now?" one of the men asked.

"She's running with a dangerous gang. You can't do that without putting yourself in danger. What we don't know is whether Joyce has figured out what these guys are doing, soup to nuts. She's a smart woman, so I think it's likely she knows exactly what's going on," he said.

My head was pounding, as much from the dust I was breathing as from the news I was hearing.

"Where do we go from here?" asked another man in the room.

"We believe there's a drop coming in Palo Duro Canyon tomorrow night," said the colonel. "We will be there in force. It's our first clear chance to catch these guys in the act. Report to the staging area outside the canyon at fifteen hundred hours tomorrow."

I watched the meeting breaking up. Then, realizing we had to get out of the building immediately, I crawled backward as fast as I could manage and dropped down to the ledge. We didn't have time to reset the grate over the hole, so we had to take our chances on that.

"Come on," I said, "we have only a few seconds before they'll come pouring out of that room."

We streaked across the hallway and burst through the swinging doors. I heard their voices spilling into the corridor and knew we had just made it. But we still had to get out of the building and across the parking lot without anyone noticing. As we raced down the four floors to the basement, my heart was beating so hard I thought I might faint. We were calling it close.

"Watch out," Rachel hissed in a loud whisper, grabbing Jane and me just as we were about to head for the door to the outside.

Someone, a man in overalls, had come inside and worked to open up the huge double doors we had come through. A huge trash truck backed slowly up to the building. We could see now that the enormous trash containers for the building lined the walls.

"Now what?" Rachel whispered.

"I guess we have to wait it out," I said.

"And hope we don't get locked in here," Jane said.

We huddled in a corner for what seemed like forever but was probably twenty minutes, while the trash process finished. We held our breath as the man in overalls walked outside, shut the big double doors, and, unmistakably, locked them tight.

"Oh, boy," Rachel said.

In total darkness, except for the sliver of light at the end of the corridor, we sat motionless, our hands intertwined, stunned.

"We have to go out the front door," Jane said finally.

We kept our hands clasped as we made our way through the dark and back to the swinging doors. I poked my head inside to make sure the coast was clear. It was quiet on this level, but we would have to go up one floor to get to the front door. I looked at my watch. It had been about half an hour since the meeting ended.

"Let's see if we can find a window where we can look out at where their cars were parked," I said. "See if they're all gone."

Once we were on the first floor, which was all quiet, we found a window. We saw two officers standing next to a patrol car. We watched them until they got into the car and drove away.

"I think that's all of them," Rachel said. "Should we run for it?"

We pushed the door open, ran down the grand steps of the courthouse and into the parking lot. We jumped inside and Jane fired up the engine. She got us out of the lot as quickly and safely as possible, and as we motored down the highway back toward the canyon, we all sat silent, in shock over what we'd just pulled off.

CHAPTER FOURTEEN

Rachel broke the silence. "I'm hoping that was all worth it. What did you find out?"

I told them what I'd heard, ending with the part about the big bust they expected to make in the canyon the next night.

"Wow," Jane said. "Your mom might be there?"

"Yeah, I guess so. I don't know. I'm so mixed up."

Rachel leaned over the seat from the back. "That lady cop told us to get out of here, but I think we should stay. I can talk my dad into letting me spend one more night at Jane's. This could be our big break."

"You're right," I said. "Jane?"

"I agree. I'm just thinking we need some equipment. We'll need binoculars and a decent camera or two for taking pictures, documenting what we see."

"Of course!" I said. "There's a place in Amarillo where we can get that stuff. But how would we pay for it?"

Jane pulled off the road, preparing to turn back. "I have a credit card," she said.

I gave Jane directions on how to get to the camera and electronics shop I knew about because of Dad's photography hobby. We bought the cameras and binoculars we needed, as well as a set of walkie-talkies.

"I feel like Agent 99," Rachel said, testing the walkie-talkies.

It was already dark when we drove back into the canyon. When we got to the site, we left the equipment in the trunk of the car.

"Are y'all as nervous as I am?" I asked as we set up for supper.

"This is the most exciting thing that's ever happened to me in my whole life," Rachel said.

"I have to admit, I never would have predicted this much excitement out here in the middle of nowhere," Jane said, holding a hot dog over the fire.

I picked up a handful of mini marshmallows and tossed them at Jane. "You thought we were just a bunch of hicks, didn't ya!"

"Well, uh, yeah, and you think that's changed?"

I jumped across the firepit and took Jane into a roll across the camp floor, pinning her to the ground on her back.

"Panhandle hicks, huh? You might want to show some respect..."

Jane pulled a move and got me on my back. "Let's see who's showing who what," Jane said, her face close to mine.

"Okay, ladies, I think this calls for an arm wrestling match. That's the only way we're gonna settle this," said Rachel, trying to separate us.

Jane let up on me and we set up the match with our arms on a rock, Rachel officiating. When Rachel gave the signal, I took an early lead, forcing Jane's arm back twenty degrees. But Jane came back strong. We were at a straight-up impasse for several seconds until finally Jane relaxed just enough for me to finish her off.

"God almighty," Jane said. "You are stronger than you look."

"Those bad guys don't know what they're up against," said Rachel, only half kidding.

"Hey, Rachel," Jane said, "do you mind holding down the fort while Cal and I take a walk?"

"Sure," Rachel said, crossing her arms. "No problem. That's what I do. Hold down the fort. Yep."

"Don't be like that," I said.

"I just want to stretch my legs a little," Jane said, reaching her hand out to help me up.

"I'll be here," Rachel said as Jane and I sauntered off.

"Where to?" I asked as we headed out to the Park Road.

"Let's head toward the Trading Post," Jane said. "Maybe I'll buy you something." She winked at me.

It was a clear night, the stars sparkling in the sky like a sea of Christmas lights. We walked in silence for a while, the cool, dry night air chilling our faces.

"Feels kinda like the calm before the storm," I said.

Jane nodded in agreement. "Eerie."

I stopped and turned to her, touching her arm for a second. "It means a lot to me that you're here."

She smiled and the moon spotlighted her face in a way that gave me goose bumps.

"Not just that you're here now, but that you moved here."

"I get it," Jane said. "Me too."

"So…" I said, kicking at the dirt, all of a sudden feeling shy.

"Hey," Jane said, catching my hand. "That woman. Bev. The cop."

"What about her?"

"Did you think she was…a little friendly? To you, I mean?"

"Uhh…hmm. Maybe? But why?"

"I don't know. She seemed nice, though. Pretty."

"Pretty? I guess so. I didn't really notice."

"C'mon. I said I was going to buy you a present," Jane said, pulling me toward the Trading Post. "Let's see what they've got in there."

We browsed through the Texas tourist souvenirs, which included a little book called *Texas Braggs*, a collection of corny Texas sayings and jokes. Jane thought it was so funny that she bought a copy.

"Texans," she said, closing the book. "You're all so proud."

"Didn't you have fifth grade Texas history?"

"I was in California for fifth grade."

"Well, if you had taken Texas history, you would know why we're all so proud," I said, laughing.

"Look," Jane said, pointing to an arrowhead decorated with fake red and purple jewels.

"Do you like it?"

"It's really pretty," I said as I turned it over in my hand.

"Then that's what I'm buying you," she announced, taking it from my hand.

When we settled down to sleep that night, I put the arrowhead under my pillow.

The next morning we sat around our cold campfire to talk about our secret plan.

"First off, we have to pull a fast one and pretend we broke camp and got out of here like Officer Gillette told us to. Otherwise, they'll probably have the park rangers kick us out," I said.

"How are we gonna do that?" Rachel asked.

"I have an idea," I said. "But it's tricky. And if we mess it up, this whole caper is done."

"What is it?" Jane asked.

"We move our campsite over to that area behind the dump station where no one ever goes because it smells."

"Eeuuww, yuck," Rachel said.

"But first, we drive to the exit and go out, and then stop and have Rachel distract that ranger at the gate, Missy, with some nonsense about going into HQ one more time. Meanwhile, we turn back around and sneak in."

"What about me? How do I get back in?" Rachel asked.

"You're gonna have to use your charms. You tell her you dropped a ring or something out the window a little way back and you need to go look for it. It'll be close to the end of her shift, so hopefully she'll just forget about you and go on home."

"I don't know, Cal. That sounds iffy to me," Rachel said.

"Well, if y'all can think of something better, great. But that's the best I can do."

"I think you can pull it off, Rachel. You're so clever," Jane said. "I like it."

Rachel glowed. "You're right. Okay. I'll do it."

"We have to assume the Rangers will be in here tonight, trying to catch these folks and maybe even make an arrest," I said.

"Right," said Jane.

"We don't want to mess that up," Rachel said.

"No, we don't. So we have to stay out of sight. Once we're back in here, no one can know it."

And so we followed the plan. We packed everything up in the car and drove to the exit.

"Bye!" we all hollered at the same time.

We waved and made a big deal out of our departure.

"Be careful out there, girls!" Missy called as we passed.

As soon as we got outside, Rachel jumped out and went back to talk to Missy. Sure enough, she got Missy to leave her post and we rolled back in as quickly as we could. Rachel showed up a little while later.

"No problemo," she said, giving me and Jane a high-five each.

We were settled into our new smelly quarters by dinnertime. We decided we should try to get some sleep in the early evening since we might be up all night. We were so keyed up that it was hard to force ourselves to sleep for a few hours before midnight. But we finally just lay down and set the alarm for eleven thirty. When it went off, I was so groggy I couldn't remember what was going on or even where I was.

"Man," I said. "I was so deep asleep."

We got up and dressed in the green fatigues we'd picked up in an army surplus store in Amarillo. By the time I was outfitted, I was wide awake. I pulled out the map.

"Let's go over our positions," I said. "Rachel, you'll be here," I said, pointing to the playground. "See if you can get on top of something high up."

"Where do you want me?" Jane asked.

"Over here," I said, "at the Lone Star Theater. You should have a good view from the top of the building. I'll be at the dump station."

We tied back our hair and pulled black-knit face masks over our heads—something Rachel had come up with in the five-and-dime store. We tested all of the equipment and made sure we could hear each other over the walkie-talkies.

"Okay, ladies," I said. "Listen up. What we're about to do is very dangerous. You heard how the Rangers described these people. All we want to do tonight is get some pictures, right?"

Jane and Rachel nodded in agreement.

"No funny business," I said, giving Rachel the hairy eyeball.

"I've got it," Rachel said.

"Okay, take your positions!"

We walked as quickly as we could to our posts. It was just after midnight. Using my binoculars, I kept an eye on the area where we expected the tanker to show up. At a quarter to one, I saw someone walking into that spot—a man dressed in dark clothes and a baseball cap. I radioed Jane.

"Do you see that guy?"

"I do. He may be a lookout."

Rachel piped in, "There's another guy. He's signaling a thumbs-up. I'm taking pictures."

At that moment, a bus-size RV pulled in. I took shot after shot, hoping to capture something, anything.

"Jane, what do you see?" I whispered into my radio.

"The two men got into the bus. It's just idling now. Nothing is happening."

We kept watch as the minutes ticked by. It was getting close to two a.m. and nothing else had happened.

"Do you think they called it off?" Rachel asked.

"No reason to think that," I said. "Just hold tight. They have plenty of time before sunrise."

"Wait," Jane said, "I see trucks. It looks like three of them."

"Everyone get your cameras out," I ordered.

One of the trucks pulled up to the side of the bus. I could see someone connecting what looked like a large hose to the tanker. I snapped a picture.

"Can anyone see faces?" I asked.

"Not really," Jane answered.

"I got a look at the bus driver," Rachel said.

"How close are you?"

"I'm on top of the swing set."

"Did you get his face on camera?"

"I think so—ouch, oops!"

I heard a crash. I grabbed my binoculars. The men had heard it too. They were scrambling and heading in the direction of the playground. I grabbed the walkie-talkie.

"Plan B, Plan B!" I barked.

I took my radio and the rest of my equipment and ran as fast as I could to the Goodnight Dugout, where we had agreed to meet if things got out of hand. It was up Park Road about fifty yards from Hackberry. Jane was right behind me.

"Come on, Rachel," I said, "you better get over here."

We had practiced the route in the dark. Rachel had run it the fastest.

"Maybe we should go back for her," Jane said.

"Give it another minute," I said. "If they got her…"

Just then, Rachel came sliding into the dugout, out of breath and pouring sweat.

"Thank God," I said.

"What happened?" Jane asked.

"I lost my balance. I fell off the swing set," she said. "I dropped my walkie-talkie. I tried to find it…but I had to get out of there."

"Did they get a look at you?" I said.

"I don't think so."

"Jane, keep a lookout for a while, so we know they didn't follow us."

Jane took her binoculars to the entrance of the dugout. She lay down, propped up on the elbows, looking through the glasses.

"Hold on," Jane said. "I can see someone coming up the road with a flashlight."

"Can you describe them at all?"

"Oh, yeah," Jane said quietly.

"What?"

"He's wearing a khaki uniform and a cowboy hat. Sort of looks like the same uniform as all the Texas Rangers we've seen. He must be one of them."

"Dang," I said, "I bet we've messed up their bust. I think we're in big trouble."

Jane hurried to the back of the dugout, motioning to Rachel and me. "Back here as far as we can until he goes by."

We saw his boots as he walked by the dugout. He paused for a few seconds, but it felt like forever. We held hands, breathing as quietly as we could. We waited several more minutes and then Jane crawled to the dugout entrance to take another look. She signaled the all clear.

"I think we should stay here for the night," I said. "It's too dangerous for us to try to get back to our camp now."

As we lay on the dugout's dirt floor, I gazed at the other two, who had both fallen asleep almost instantly, their gentle breathing soothing my jangled nerves. I thanked my lucky stars for them—the best friends ever.

CHAPTER FIFTEEN

We woke up stiff the next morning from sleeping on the hard clay. We had worn our civilian clothes under the army fatigues. We rolled up the fatigues and stowed them in a sleeping bag cover. We did the same with the boots. We packed the cameras, binoculars, and walkie- talkies (less Rachel's) in the third sleeping bag cover. Then we each carried one out of the dugout.

"We should try to find my walkie-talkie," Rachel said. "I can't believe I dropped it. I guess I'm not quite ready for Ranger basic training."

"I didn't realize you were planning on joining the force," I said.

"You never know."

"Well, anyway, keep your eyes open for anything out of place," I said.

We headed back toward the playground where she had lost the radio. We heard a truck engine humming in the background. I stopped short, my heart racing.

"What if they're still here?" Rachel asked.

"Didn't the Rangers say the gang would be out of here before sunrise?" Jane asked me.

"That's right. But look." I pointed to a clearing over the horizon. "That's one of the RVs they pulled in here last night. They're still here."

"We have to be cool as cucumbers," Jane said. "They have no reason to believe we're a threat."

"Be cool," I said. "And forget about that walkie-talkie."

We continued down the road at a leisurely pace and passed Hackberry. We saw the RV up close. There were several men standing around, talking with their heads down, really serious. These guys were definitely not Rangers. I noticed one of them had Rachel's walkie-talkie in his hand. He looked up and saw us, but looked back without missing a beat.

"Let's make small talk with each other and not make eye contact with them," I said.

We chitchatted as we walked until we got back to our own campsite.

"Oh, my, God," Rachel said, slumping to the ground in a heap.

"That was way too close a call," I said. "We need to get out of here."

As we packed up our tent and the rest of our things, I spotted the man I'd seen holding the walkie-talkie coming toward us with two other men.

"Heads up," I said to Jane and Rachel.

As they approached us, the lead man gave us the once-over before he said anything.

"Mornin' ladies," he said in a fake, friendly tone.

"What can we do for you?" I asked, stepping forward.

"We're lookin' for somebody who lost something."

He held up the walkie-talkie.

"Know who this belongs to?" he asked, his eyes narrowing.

"I've never seen one of those before in real life," Rachel said, attempting to take it from him.

He pulled the device away and looked at her for a few seconds before turning to Jane and me.

"I have no idea," I said.

"Me neither," said Jane.

"Hope you find 'em," Rachel said, continuing to pack up.

"You girls leavin'?"

"We have to get back. School and all," I said. "Have a nice day."

The men finally walked on.

"Good job, y'all," I said.

We finished loading up the car and headed out of the canyon. Jane didn't say a word for miles.

"Hey, what's wrong? Other than we just almost got killed by those dangerous criminals."

Jane frowned. "Right. And I'm the one who is responsible for that."

"What do you mean?" Rachel and I asked almost at the exact same time.

"I'm the oldest. I agreed to get us all this equipment and I should have known we could get ourselves into a lot of trouble," she said. "I don't know what I was thinking. This was way too dangerous."

"Jane, it's not your fault," I said. "Rachel and I are almost as old as you. And, anyway, we're all in this together."

"Yeah, we're on our way home now. So everything's okay, right?" Rachel said.

"Okay, fair enough," Jane said. "But I don't mind telling you, what happened in there scared me to death."

We were all quiet as we drove along the flat, dusty panhandle highway. As we approached a Motel 6 off the road into Amarillo, Jane thought she saw something suspicious. I took out a pair of the binoculars and scanned the area. What I saw worried me. A lot.

"It's the Texas Rangers," I said. "They've set up a roadblock. They're stopping cars."

"We're not driving into that," Jane said.

"No, we're not. Let's take this turn," I said.

"Officer Gillette wouldn't like it if she found out we didn't leave the canyon like we were supposed to," Rachel said.

"Yeah, let's hope they didn't notice us just now," I said. "We messed up their chance to catch those guys. We don't want them to figure that out."

We turned off on a narrow dirt road and drove a few miles. I kept watch through the binoculars in case anyone had spotted us.

"So far, so good," I said after half an hour.

"Let's look at the map," Jane said, pulling off the road.

"This road will hook us back on to 387 and we can get home from there," Rachel said, pointing out the route.

"I don't know," I said. "The more I think about it, the more I'm not so sure about going back home now. What if we accidentally left a clue back there in the camp? The Rangers could figure it out. The gang could figure it out."

"You're right," Jane agreed.

"We could go to Sweetwater," I said.

"To your grandmother's place." Jane nodded. "How do we get there?"

I showed them where Sweetwater was on the map, west of Abilene.

"It's pretty much a straight shot south. Should take about four hours," I said.

"We need to get a new tire. The spare won't make it that far."

"Okay," I said. "Let me think. There should be a good service station in Plainview or Floydada."

"Let's stay off the main highways, even if it takes a little longer," Jane said.

Rachel took the map and started planning a back roads route. "I think Floydada's better for staying on the back roads."

"Let's do it," Jane said.

"I can't believe we're running from the Texas Rangers now," Rachel said, as she wrote out the turns for Jane.

"I just want to get somewhere safe so we can take a breath and figure out what's going on," I said.

"I'd really like to see those photographs we took," Jane said.

"Me too," I said. "We can get them developed in Sweetwater."

The first service station we found didn't take credit cards, but he told us there was a station in Paducah that did. It was a little out of our way, but what choice did we have? I dozed off as the sun pierced the windshield. I had a dream that Mom was driving a tanker truck and careening down a highway. The truck was about to go off a cliff when I woke up screaming, "No!"

"Hey," Jane said, grabbing my hand. "It's okay. You were dreaming."

"Oh my God. My mother was about to die."

"We'll find her," Jane said. "I know we will."

I collapsed back against the seat, visions of my mother being roughed up by three big thugs in cowboy boots. How had she been dragged into something like this?

Luckily the repair shop in Paducah wasn't busy, and they had the tire we needed. But the gas line was forever. We had to wait behind a dozen cars and trucks for about half an hour. It was the OPEC oil embargo. You could never be sure you would even get gas. Sometimes the pumps ran dry. This time we were okay. Rachel and I had enough money to buy Cokes and Fritos for a snack. We were starting to feel really guilty about using Jane's credit card all the time. I picked up a newspaper while I was in the filling station.

"Hey, look at this," I said to Jane, showing her the newspaper.

"What is it?" Rachel asked, getting into the backseat.

"It's a picture of Jane's dad, and the headline says, 'Harold Rawlings greets Congressman Wells at Washington, D.C. Petroleum Summit.'"

"So, that's where your parents are," I said.

"Wow, your dad's a big deal!" Rachel said.

"Yeah, I guess so," Jane said with a shrug.

"Does he have anything to do with OPACK?" Rachel said.

"O-P-E-C," I said, spelling it out for her. "Organization of Petroleum Exporting Countries."

"Whatever," Rachel said. "Why do you have to be so precise about everything all the time?"

"I know he has something to do with it," Jane replied, "but I'm not really sure exactly how. You know he works at the same company both your dads do."

"I kinda thought that. Is he their boss?" Rachel said.

"Technically, I guess. But I think there are quite a few people in between them."

"What she's saying, Rachel, is that our dads are peons and her dad is the head honcho."

"That's not what I'm saying."

"Well, that's the way it is. And that's okay. You shouldn't feel embarrassed or anything."

It was late afternoon as we pulled across the railroad tracks that separated the road from Grandma's farm. We approached the cattle guard and the gated fence that stood at the entrance to the property. I opened the gate and we drove up to the house. Grandma was on the porch when we got there.

It was a two-story farmhouse built out of a sandy-colored brick. The porch wrapped around three sides and two wooden rocking chairs sat near the front door with a table between them. She had dozens of flowerpots and cacti scattered on the porch and steps. An old, out-of-commission outhouse sat a few yards away from the house. A dilapidated barn stood behind it, the paint faded and chipped. Behind the house, and in every direction, were miles of red dirt covered in bits of grass and the occasional tumbleweed.

"What in tarnation!" Grandma put her hands on her hips and shook her head as the three of us spilled out of the car.

"Sorry we didn't let you know," I said, giving her a hug.

"That's okay. Come on inside. I was just about to get dinner on the table."

We brought a few things in from the car and helped Grandma set the table.

"Now, first of all," Grandma said, "unless I'm mistaken, you girls are supposed to be in school right about now."

Jane and Rachel looked at me and said nothing.

"Yes, that's true. Technically. But something more important has come up and we need your help."

"Do tell," Grandma said. "I'm more than a little curious about what y'all have been up to. But before we get to that, I'm calling your dad, young lady, and letting him know I'm sending you straight home first thing in the morning."

"No, Grandma, listen to me first." I almost cried.

"No, ma'am. Wait right there until I finish this call."

Grandma went into her study where she kept her telephone. She was gone longer than I thought it should have taken to have that conversation.

"Well, girls, there's been a change of plan."

I couldn't imagine what this was about. "What is it?"

"A freak tornado hit Dumas this morning. I haven't had the TV or radio on all day, so I had no idea. It hit your high school hard. There won't be any school for at least a week."

"Oh my god," the three of us said, almost in unison.

"I told your dad I would keep you here until things get sorted out. He's going to let your folks know. So, I guess we're on a slumber party for now."

Over dinner, we told our Palo Duro Canyon stories and filled her in about the Brazos River Gang, the Texas Rangers, and what little we knew about Mom.

"I have to say," Grandma said, "sounds like my daughter has got herself up a tree."

"Grandma, can you go to town tomorrow and get this film developed? We hope there's something we can use."

"I know a place. They can get it done in a few hours."

"Can we just watch some TV tonight?" Rachel asked. "I need a break. My head hurts from all this stuff."

"Best idea ever," Jane said.

We sat in our pajamas in front of the TV for a couple of hours that night watching *I Dream of Jeannie* and *Bewitched*, and of course some *Perry Mason*, before we said our goodnights. Jane and I went up to the loft bedroom at the top of a narrow set of wooden stairs. There was one narrow, double bed.

"You better stay on your side," Jane said as she pushed me over toward the wall.

"Don't worry about that," I said. "Just don't steal the covers."

CHAPTER SIXTEEN

We played poker and hearts and authors while we waited for Grandma to get back with the developed photos. As soon as she walked through the door, we grabbed the package and laid them out on the kitchen table. A lot of them were blurry or too dark to make out the images, but one caught my eye.

"Is there a magnifying glass?"

"Here you go," Grandma said, taking one out of the kitchen drawer.

I held the magnifying glass up to the photo, looking at it carefully. At first, I thought I was seeing things. But I wasn't. I couldn't help it. I buried my head between my knees and let out an ugly scream.

"What is it?"

Rachel grabbed the glass and looked for herself.

"Oh my God, it's Joyce!" she said. "She was driving that RV!"

"No!" Grandma cried.

I felt like someone had punched me. Jane looked at the photo like she didn't believe it.

"It doesn't mean she's working with them voluntarily," Jane said, kneeling next to me. "Don't jump to any conclusions. This is just one piece of information."

"What now, then?" I asked. We sat there, stunned and quiet for several seconds, until I couldn't stand it any longer. "I need to get out of here for a while. Clear my head."

"Do you mind if I come?" Jane asked. "You can show me around. Take your mind off this for a while."

"Sure," I said. "I'd love to."

Rachel looked at me and I knew what she was thinking. She had figured out that I had a crush on Jane. I had been waiting for her to confront me, but she was holding back for some reason. Sooner or later, though, she would do a Come to Jesus with me. I knew it.

I looked away and walked out the side screen door. Jane followed. We walked past the barn and across a pasture. The grass was spotty and the rocky terrain made for slow going. They'd had a drought here for most of the year. Tumbleweeds blew by, piling up against fences of scrawny mesquite trees. I loved this place. The simplicity of it was its own form of beauty. I always felt calm here, peaceful and protected. We walked for a long time without saying anything. We got to the creek. A thin stream of water barely covered the rocks across the bottom. They were slick, polished by decades of exposure. Jane slipped on one and stumbled toward the opposite bank, but I caught her arm and kept her from hitting the ground.

"Good catch," she said, breaking the silence.

"You think you know someone," I said, "and then they do something completely out of nowhere and you realize you don't know them at all."

Jane nodded and a nearby cow surprised us with a long, low moo, as if agreeing with me. We both laughed.

"No matter what," Jane said, "she's your mother."

We walked across the dusty landscape as the wind picked up and blew red dirt into our faces.

"The tank's over here," I said, pointing to the north. "We can wash off."

We approached a small body of water, a pond in the ground. "Why do they call it a tank?" Jane asked.

"Because it's man-made. They usually block off a stream so the water pools. They make it so it traps rainwater too."

We knelt and splashed water on our faces and necks. I took off my overshirt and handed it to Jane while my camisole clung to my skin.

"Sorry there's no towels. Just use this," I said.

I felt Jane's eyes lingering on my bare shoulders as she used the shirt to dry her face and neck.

"Here," she said, holding the shirt out so I could put my arms through the sleeves. I let her put the shirt back on me. Then she slowly buttoned the shirt from behind, her arms around me. She pulled my hair to one side and breathed deeply at the nape of my neck. I tingled everywhere. I leaned back against her as she buttoned the last button. She hugged me tightly and then let me go.

"Thank you," I said, turning to look at her.

"You're very welcome."

"I guess we should get back," I said, but I didn't move. I wanted her to say no. I wanted more of whatever just happened. I wanted it, but I couldn't ask for it.

"It's dinnertime," she said.

"Right."

The four of us were quiet around the dinner table, trying to make sense of the bizarre facts we had uncovered. I could tell Grandma was thinking differently about Mom, as was I. We both had trouble putting words to it, but it was like she was no longer her daughter or my mother. She was some stranger in trouble.

"Hey," I said, shaking myself out of a trance. "What if we got in touch with Officer Gillette?"

"That's an idea," Rachel said.

"She said we should call if we hear anything or see anything. Do you think she would be mad about what we did in the canyon?"

"Who is this you're talking about?" Grandma asked.

"She's a Texas Ranger. She's the one who told us about the meeting in Amarillo," I said.

"I don't know," Jane said. "What if she decides to arrest us? I think we should test her first."

"How?" I asked.

"Well," Jane said, "Mrs. Norman, you could call her and say you have some information about Hank Hart, but you want to meet her—only her. Then you ask her to come to a certain place in Sweetwater."

"Okay," I said, "but Grandma, you have to use a fake name. Otherwise, she might figure out that we're here and they'll come for us."

"You think this'll work?" Grandma asked.

"Well," Jane said, "if she comes alone, you can bring her back here. If not, you call us and we'll get out of here."

"I think it's worth a shot," I said.

Grandma made the call and arranged the meeting for the next day. "She was curious how I got her number, but I tap danced around that."

"Was she suspicious of anything?"

"I couldn't tell," Grandma said. "She was playing it close to the vest."

"She's coming alone?" I asked.

"I told her I wouldn't approach her if I saw anyone else around."

"Okay, well, we have a plan," I said.

"Why are you acting like I'm not here?" Rachel asked as we stood washing the supper dishes.

I looked at her blankly. "What?"

"You know what I mean. Right now. You're acting like I'm not here because you don't want to talk about what's going on."

"All we've been doing is talking about what's going on."

"Stop it, Cal. You know I'm not talking about the stuff with your mom."

I sighed. I crossed my arms and gave her an exasperated look. I still thought I might be able to put her off.

"What are we talking about then?"

"Jane."

I blinked a few times. I held my stance. I didn't look away. "What about Jane?"

She narrowed her eyes and I started to crack. I turned to the sink, looking out the window. If we were going to talk about this, I couldn't look her in the eye.

"Are you in love with her?"

"What?" That knocked the wind out of me.

"You're acting like you're in love."

"No," I said. *What if she's right?* I couldn't make sense of it. "I just like her. I thought you were going to say you didn't like her getting in the middle of us."

"You're full of it, Cal. There's something going on there and you know it. And I don't like it that you won't talk to me about it."

I couldn't come up with a response so I just stood there, staring blankly at her. She threw the dishtowel in the sink and stormed out. I finished the dishes by myself. What the heck? I pushed the "in love" thing out, but it kept coming back.

* * *

I felt shaky when I got into bed with Jane, almost like I was doing something wrong, sinful.

"You know," Jane said, skooching under the covers. "Earlier, at the tank—" She suddenly hesitated.

"Yeah? What about it?"

"I just…I don't know. I don't want you to feel uncomfortable."

I turned to face her. "What do you mean? Why would I feel uncomfortable?"

"Do you not want to talk about it?"

I looked away. "It's…it's hard for me."

"I understand. Let's go to sleep."

She rolled over.

"I've been feeling this way for…a while," I said.

"Feeling what way?"

"Like…hmm…like I want to kiss you but…"

Now I'd done it. My heart pounded and I started to sweat. Jane turned back to me and came a little closer. She put her hand on my thigh, her breathing quicker and heavier.

"But what?"

"I also feel like…like it's not right. I mean, that it's wrong."

"For two girls to kiss," Jane said.

"Right. Kissing…would be wrong."

"Just kissing?"

Jane's lips hovered close, so close, almost touching. But I turned away quickly, pulling the covers over my head.

"Ohmygod, ohmygod, ohmygod," I said. "I'm sorry. I'm so sorry. I'm such a loser."

Jane turned away from me and sighed in exasperation. I felt about as lame and ridiculous as I had ever felt. Why didn't I just do it? I wanted to, but I had to stop myself, right? If I did it, if I was the one who went for it, I couldn't pretend I didn't know what I was doing. I couldn't deny that I had these feelings. I was so exhausted from all of it. I couldn't think anymore. I slept without dreaming.

CHAPTER SEVENTEEN

When the sun broke through the curtains and startled me awake, Jane was spooning me, and as we stirred, we both sat up without looking at each other.

"How did you sleep?" I asked, jumping out of bed.

"Cal, look at me."

I hesitated, then turned to face her. I flushed when I caught a glimpse of her panties as she pushed off the sheets to get out of bed. I had to resist the urge to run out of the room.

"Let's take it easy," she said. "Take a deep breath. We have a lot to deal with today."

All I could do was nod, grab my clothes and run for the bathroom.

Downstairs at breakfast, we were tense and excited for Grandma's meeting. I was just happy that it meant I had something to think about other than how I felt about Jane.

"We need to pack up just in case we have to get out of Dodge," I said.

"Okay, ladies," Grandma said, picking up her purse and keys. "Stay by the phone."

I sat next to Rachel on the couch. "Hey, I'm sorry about last night. I guess I'm just shy about that whole thing."

Rachel laughed. "I know you, Carrie Ann Long. Sooner or later, you'll talk to me."

Before an hour was up, the phone rang. I jumped for it.

"Grandma?" I said into the receiver. "What happened?"

"She's willing to come," Grandma said. "And she'll come alone. We'll be there soon."

"It's a go?" said Jane.

"They're on their way."

"What exactly are we going to ask her to do?" Rachel said.

"She seemed cool when we met her in the canyon. I want to show her the photos and see what they mean to her. Maybe what we saw will help them find my mom."

It wasn't long before we heard wheels on the gravel in the driveway. I stepped to the window, lifting the curtain away.

"It's them."

Rachel stood stiff like a statue. "What if she knows about that stunt I pulled at the canyon to sneak back in? Do you think she might arrest me?" she whispered.

"She doesn't care about that," I whispered back. "That's park rangers. She's a Texas Ranger. It's a whole different thing. Don't worry."

Bev came into Grandma's living room, dressed in pants, a blouse, and black loafers, with an air of authority that made me warm to her again. Her short brown hair fell just below her ears. She looked like an athlete, maybe a runner.

"Come on in," I said, standing and shaking her hand like a grown-up. "Thank you for coming."

"Could I get you some iced tea?" Grandma asked.

"Thank you. I'd like that."

Grandma went into the kitchen as the three of us sat there silent, waiting for Bev to say something.

"You girls did want me to come here, right?"

"Right," I said. "We're a little nervous."

"I can understand that. You've been very busy since I saw you last."

I was pretty sure she was scolding us. "What do you mean?" I asked. *What if they know we spied on the meeting?*

"We know you went out on your own in the canyon—"

"Well, of course you do," Rachel said. "You are the Texas Rangers!"

"Yes, well, what you did was extremely dangerous. You could have been hurt. Or worse."

"I know," Jane said. "I can't forgive myself for letting Cal and Rachel take a chance like that."

"Jane, stop," I said. "It was my idea," I said to Bev.

"You were lucky. Something disrupted them that night. We don't know what."

I looked away. I didn't dare make eye contact with Jane or Rachel.

"Now," Bev went on, "Mrs. Norman says you have something you want to talk to me about."

"We have something to show you, but before we do, I have a few questions I'd like to ask if that's okay with you," I said.

"If I can give you an answer, I will."

"Okay," I said.

I could sense Jane and Rachel tense up beside me, like they were worried I was going to get us further in a hole.

I stood, pacing around the room like I'd seen Perry Mason do. "Who planted that photo of Hackberry Camp in my mailbox?"

"Yeah," Rachel said. "That's what took us to Palo Duro Canyon in the first place."

"Excellent question," Bev said. "The key question, in fact." She stood as if to add authority to her words. "It was none other than Hank Hart."

We all looked at each other, confused.

"But—" I said.

"Why would he do that?" Jane asked.

"And how do you know?" Rachel chimed in.

Bev took a deep breath. "I've been the agent in charge of following Hank Hart for the last two years. I've never met him, but I feel like I know him better than I know most of my family."

"Go on," Grandma said.

"He really fell hard for your daughter," she said to Grandma. "That's caused him to go a little soft. Make a few mistakes."

"You're saying he dropped the photo in my mailbox so I could find her?"

"I think he'd like to get her out of harm's way, but he can't do it himself. He has to convince his sons and the other men that he's loyal to the operation above all. And willing to sacrifice Joyce if necessary."

"You said he's made some mistakes," I said.

"One of my guys was following him when he made that drop at your house," Bev said, looking at me. "He was alone, which is unusual, so we kept an eye on your house for a while. That's how we realized y'all were up to something."

"Officer Gillette—"

"Please, call me Bev."

"Okay, Bev. We were looking at the pictures we took in the canyon that night."

"What? If you took pictures, you may have captured what happened to disrupt the fuel drop!"

The three of us looked at each other, unsure of what to say.

"It was me," Rachel said, looking at the floor. "I caused a ruckus and they ran scared, dropped everything."

Bev stood up and I could tell she was furious. "Do you realize what you've done? We prepared for that stakeout for the last six months. I had a big promotion riding on that bust. I should haul you all off to jail right this minute."

"Oh, my goodness," Grandma said, her hands at her heart. "This is very unfortunate. What can the girls do to make this up to you?"

"Please," I said. "We really were just trying to help, in what now seems like an obviously stupid way. I wanted to find my mom. That's all. Isn't it possible that the photos we got that night could help you build your case against the gang?"

"Yeah!" Rachel chimed in. "We found one that shows Cal's mother driving the RV."

"Okay. That's interesting," Bev said, softening a bit. "What else did you get?"

We went into the kitchen and emptied a box full of photos onto the dining table. Bev went through them carefully.

"These are some excellent shots of the tankers and the RV. I can even see the connection between them. You seem to have had a better vantage point than our cameras did that night."

"So, we did help, after all," Jane said.

Bev nodded. She then examined the picture of Joyce through the magnifying glass.

"Does it mean she's part of the gang?" Grandma asked.

"It's impossible to know for sure at this point," Bev said. "She may be going along with things for now because she's in over her head. Or maybe they've promised her something that makes it worth the risk."

"Maybe she's got Stockholm Syndrome," Rachel said.

"What? Where do you come up with these things?" I said.

"It's where a hostage starts to identify with her captors," Bev said. "It happened this summer in a high-profile case in Sweden."

Rachel smirked at me.

"Well, anyway," I said, "I'm sorry, real sorry, we messed up your chance to get Hart the other night. What do you think they will do next?"

Bev sat back in her chair, obviously thinking about the question carefully before responding. "I know your motive is pure. You want to find your mom. But you need to stay out of this, Cal. I mean it. I'm taking these photos with me to Ft. Worth. Just get back to school where you belong."

"No, please! That's not fair. The pictures are our property," I said as I ran to gather them up into my arms.

"You're wrong. They're evidence in a criminal investigation. Now put them down."

I was furious and started crying I was so mad. "I wish we had never met you."

"Calm down," Grandma said. "Everything's going to be okay, Cal. They're going to find your mother."

"Right," I said, sneering. "I'll believe it when I see it."

Jane and Rachel stood on either side of me, each taking an arm, trying to comfort me. I was shaking with rage. I wanted to tackle her, but all we could do was watch helplessly while Bev packed up all the photos and loaded them into her brand-new Wagoneer.

"Nice truck." Rachel whistled at the Jeep with wooden side panels and a chrome grille. I glared at her like she was sympathizing with the enemy. "Well, it is," she said.

Bev drove off as the four of us watched the Jeep disappear, the red dust swirling in its trail. I felt someone had punched me and knocked the wind out of me.

CHAPTER EIGHTEEN

Rachel, Jane, and I stood staring at each other, helpless, mute, while Grandma looked on from the porch.

"Why don't you girls get back inside. I'll make us an apple pie and some homemade ice cream. Let the Rangers do their job and I'm sure this will all be okay in the end."

Dejected, having no idea what to do next, I signaled to the other two that we might as well go inside. Grandma went to work in the kitchen, and realizing how crushed we were, didn't even make us help. We went up to the room Jane and I shared so we could talk in private.

"This is the worst," I said. "We're totally cut out."

"I guess we should have known she wasn't going to let us in on their investigation. It was really dumb to think she could," Jane said.

"There's nothing stopping us from going to Ft. Worth on our own," Rachel said, her eyes wide, as though she'd come up with a brilliant idea.

"Nothing?" I said. "Nothing except Grandma, the Texas Rangers, our parents, the school. Other than that, it's easy peasy."

"Wait a minute," Jane said as Rachel looked glumly at the floor. "Your grandmother and the Rangers aren't going to expect us to keep going on this. And the school, well, it's still closed for now since there's no water or electricity. So it looks like we won't be back in there for at least a week."

"But what about my dad? Your parents? Rachel's?"

"Here's the idea. We have to make your grandmother believe we're going back home, and at the same time, we make our parents believe we're hanging out here until the school reopens," Jane said.

"I don't know. I guess it could work. But what are we going to do in Ft. Worth?" I just couldn't shake my negative thoughts. I was so down in the dumps about what Bev had done. I had really believed she would help us and I felt like a fool for that now.

"First things first. Let's all call our folks and let them know we're going to hang out in Sweetwater for the week. They're not gonna care. My dad hates to spend money on long distance calls, so he won't call to check up on us in the meantime," Rachel said.

"We'll tell your grandmother we're headed back home in the morning. We can make a big deal out of how defeated we are and all that, so she won't suspect that we would do anything else," Jane said.

"You two sure are confident," I said, standing and pacing the room. "But this feels like a wild goose chase to me."

"Maybe," Jane said. "But one thing leads to another. Look how far we've gotten already?"

"I'm starting to feel like a Texas Ranger myself," Rachel said, jumping up on a side table and holding her arms up like she was aiming a gun.

I threw a pillow at her and she fell backward off the table, hitting her head against the wall.

"Ouch!"

"I'm sorry," I said, running to help her up. "Let's pack up. I'll let Grandma know we're headed back home first thing in the morning.

Grandma watched as we drove off toward home. Once we were on the highway, we circled back and headed in the direction of Ft. Worth. Four hours later, as we rolled into town, we spotted a phone booth and pulled over to look up the address of Arlington Heights High School. In one of Rachel's side chats with Bev, she had learned that she lived across the street from there. Rachel's habit of being nosy sometimes came in handy.

"We need a map," Jane said.

We stopped at a gas station nearby and bought a street map of Ft. Worth. The high school was easy to find, right off the interstate and closer to downtown.

"We'll need to hang around there after five, when she should be coming home from work," I said.

"I'm a little nervous," Rachel said. "What if we run into her?"

"We have to be smarter than that," I said. "Maybe there's a spot in the school parking lot where we can watch and wait."

The front of the high school faced the interstate. The parking lot was in the back and faced a row of modest single-story houses. We had to hope one of them was Bev's. As the clock ticked closer to six, I was feeling anxious, like this was yet another harebrained idea. But just then, we saw her car.

"There she is!" Rachel said as Bev's Jeep pulled into one of the houses across the street.

I looked at Rachel and Jane and realized they were thinking the same thing I was thinking.

"Okay, so now we know where she lives," I said.

"But what are we going to do?" Jane said.

"Sleep out overnight? Break in when she goes to work in the morning?" Rachel asked sheepishly.

We had been pouting for several minutes when Jane grabbed my arm. "She's leaving!"

We looked over to see Bev getting into the Jeep and driving away.

"Let's go!" I said.

We parked on the street that shared an alley with Bev's and walked as nonchalantly as we could to the back of her house.

There was a fence with an unlocked gate, so we walked in like we owned the place. The backyard was neat, the grass freshly cut and trimmed, with a deck near the back fence next to the two-car garage. An outdoor table and chairs sat on the deck.

With no signs of life, we boldly approached the house. There was no back door and all the blinds were closed on the windows that faced the backyard. We rounded the side along the driveway and saw a slightly ajar screen door. I tried the door behind it, and of course, it was locked, but there was nothing covering the glass so we could see right inside.

The view was into the kitchen, which was spotless, the linoleum floor shining.

"Look!" Rachel said, pointing. "It's a kitty."

A tubby calico cat strolled toward the door, looking us over with curiosity. She sat primly and meowed loudly.

"She has a full bowl of food," Rachel said. "I bet Bev came home just to feed her."

"At least there's no dog. That would spoil our plan," Jane said.

"What is our plan, exactly?" I said.

"We should check around for a hidden key," Jane said. "People do that all the time. In case they lock themselves out."

"But she's a Texas Ranger. Do you really think she's going to leave a key laying around?"

"No, not laying around. Hidden. We have to think like her. Where would she put it?"

"Hmm," Rachel said. "What about the garage?"

She ran to check, but both garage doors were locked.

"No dice."

I stepped back and examined the house. I noticed a metal downspout on the far side, away from the driveway and walked over to take a look. Sure enough, at the bottom, underneath the part that turned away from the house, was a key keeper with a magnet holding it in place. I opened it.

I held the key up, smiling. "We're in."

As we stood at the side door, I looked at the two of them, took a deep breath and turned the lock carefully. I could tell they had as many doubts as I did about what we were doing. Were we going too far? Was it worth it? How much trouble could we get into if we got caught?

The lock clicked and the door was open. We stepped inside and Rachel picked up the cat.

"No time for that," I said. "Let's be quick about this. If there's nothing here that helps us, we need to get out, pronto."

The house was small, only two bedrooms. The smaller bedroom was set up as an office with a desk and filing cabinets.

"If there's anything, you would think it's in here," Jane said.

I nodded. "Be careful. We don't want her to know we were here. Whatever you touch, put it back the way you found it."

We checked drawers and filing cabinets but found nothing interesting. Then Rachel opened the closet door.

"Look," she said. "Here's some boxes labeled *Brazos River Gang*."

"Wow," Jane said. "The mother lode."

"This has to be what we're looking for," I said, helping them drag the boxes out into the room.

"This is going to take a while," Jane said.

"We can't take a while. We have to move fast."

We divided up the boxes and went to work. We pored over the reports, reading logs and examining maps, trying to piece together the history of the Brazos River Gang. After a couple of hours, we sat back, discouraged, our eyes red from the effort.

"Come on, girls," Rachel said. "We can't give up. We have to live up to the Texas Ranger standard."

Jane and I sighed and we all got back to work. A few minutes later, Jane gasped.

"There's a pattern here," she said, pointing to a logbook of where the gang had been known to have various activities over the previous six months.

I looked over her shoulder at the logbook and Rachel jumped up, looking over her other shoulder.

"If you draw out these movements on the map, you see these first five entries make a star starting and ending on Palo Duro Canyon."

"Spooky," Rachel said.

"And then, if you look at the next three, which is where it stops for now, you have three points of the star."

"What does it mean?" Rachel asked.

"It looks like a kind of code," I said. "Maybe those points of the star are where they're picking up the gasoline."

"Right! So, look at this. It looks like the next place they would be is over here in Tyler," Jane said, drawing the line to the next logical point.

"Tyler—my uncle lives there. He used to work at an oil refinery there. That makes sense," said Rachel.

"What's the timing on those log entries?" I asked.

"Four days apart," Jane said. "The last entry is two days ago."

"So they could be planning a strike on that refinery in Tyler in two days."

We sat quiet for a moment, just staring at the map.

"What do we do?" Rachel asked.

"How do we know the Rangers haven't already figured this out? This is their job after all," I said.

"You would think they've looked into it, but maybe they didn't notice what I noticed. You would have to be thinking about star patterns. They're a bunch of old guys for the most part, so they don't think that way," Jane said, folding her arms with finality.

"We have to tell Bev about it," Rachel said. "No matter how mad she gets that we broke into her place."

"I agree we should tell her, on the chance they haven't figured it out, but I'm worried about surprising her when she gets home. She might go nuts and arrest us or something," I said.

We decided it was best to put everything away, back where we found it, except we left the log and the map with Jane's pencil drawing of the star on top of one box. As we skedaddled out the back gate, I caught a glimpse of Bev arriving back home. We had just made it.

We drove several blocks away and located a phone booth where we could call her. I dialed her number and waited. After the fifth ring, I was ready to put the receiver back in the cradle when I heard her voice.

"Hello?"

"Hi, Officer," I said. "It's Cal and Jane and Rachel."

"Oh, hello, girls. Is everything okay? Are you in trouble?"

"Everything's fine," I said. "We just, we, well, we have an idea for you. About the Brazos River Gang."

"Hmm," Bev said. "That's interesting. What is it?"

"I'll get to that, but, uh, there's something I have to tell you first."

I was nervous and too afraid to say it, and I could see that Rachel was itching to take the phone, so when she grabbed it, I didn't resist.

"Ma'am," Rachel said with confidence, "we were in your home tonight, going through those boxes in your closet."

"You what?" Bev cried.

"I know it wasn't right for us to go in without your permission, but, well, we did. And the important thing is, we found something. Something you need to know about, if you don't already."

"Where are you girls?" she spat.

"Don't worry about that. Just go look in your closet and get the map and the log that we left out."

I took the phone back as Rachel sneered at me, "You should let me handle this from here."

I listened for Bev to come back on the line.

"Okay, I've got it. Now what is it you think you've found?"

"See the star pattern on the map?"

I could hear the rustling of crisp paper as she opened the map.

"Yes."

"That shows the order of hits on refineries. The final point of the star, if you take it that far, is Tyler."

She was so quiet I couldn't tell if she was still on the line. "Hello?"

"I see it," she said.

"And if you look at the timing on the log, you see they should be in Tyler two days from now."

She let out a long sigh as the three of us looked at each other helplessly, waiting for some reaction.

"This looks...like something we should investigate," she said at last. "But, listen to me, like I said before, the three of you need to stay out of this. Go back home. Right now. Or I'll send a passel of squad cars to look for you." She paused. "And if you ever break into my house again, I'll personally arrest you!"

CHAPTER NINETEEN

I felt my resolve slipping away, but I didn't want the other two to know it, so as we stood silent in the phone booth, I decided to just take control and come up with a plan, any plan.

"I've read about youth hostels," I said. "I wonder if they have one here."

"You mean where we could stay the night?" Rachel asked.

"Yeah. It's getting late. And I'm not sure what we should do next. We need time to think. Regroup. Figure it out."

We looked through the Yellow Pages. Under hostels there was a listing for the YWCA in downtown Ft. Worth.

"Look, it says minimum age fifteen, females only," Jane said.

"Perfect. I hope they have room."

We called to confirm they had beds for us and drove in that direction. A parking lot on the side of the building had plenty of space, so we pulled in, parked, and unloaded our bags.

"This is fun," Rachel almost squealed. "Like camp."

"I don't know," Jane said. "Do you think it's safe? It looks kinda like skid row. What if someone steals the car?"

"It's a little dodgy, I guess, but what choice do we have?"

She couldn't argue with that, so we went inside. A woman wearing cat's eyeglasses, her hair in a bun tacked up by pickup sticks, sat at an imposing elevated reception counter, looking down on us suspiciously, smoke from her cigarette swirling above her head.

Her thick drawl seemed to pour out of her mouth like molasses. "How kin I help ye?"

"We'd like to stay the night," Rachel said, perky like she was checking into the Holiday Inn.

"Lemme see ur student IDs, so's I can verify ur illegibility."

We produced our IDs and she handed us a check-in form to fill out, which we did, before passing it back to her with the required six-dollar fee.

"That gits ya a bed, linens, and breakfast in the mornin'. Ur welcome to use the kitchen tonight if ya got somethin' to cook for dinner. But make sure you clean up like you was never there."

"Thanks," we said in unison.

"And girls," she said as we gathered up our bags, "no visitors. Especially no boys."

"Yes, ma'am." Rachel saluted.

We got settled in the dorm in the furthest corner from the restroom. There were a few others already there, mostly much older than us, and none very talkative at all.

"I'm starved," Rachel said. "I wonder if there's a grocery store near here."

"I saw a Piggly Wiggly a few blocks back," Jane said. "What if Cal stays here to watch our stuff and you and I go pick up a few things?"

"Good idea," I said. "Get some canned green beans and chicken. And some instant potatoes. And some ice cream and chocolate syrup."

"You'll be okay by yourself?" Jane touched my arm lightly and something about the way she looked at me made my breath quicken.

"Sure."

While they were gone, I poked around the dorm and checked out the showers. It was all clean enough but bare and out of date, especially the faucets. They looked like something out of the thirties, which I only knew about because of antique shows I'd been to with Grandma.

"Hey, girl," said a woman from one of the bunks. "Don't go barefoot in those showers. You'll catch athlete's foot."

"Oh," I said. "Thanks. I've had that before. It was awful."

Jane and Rachel weren't gone that long, and when they got back, Jane went down to the kitchen to put the ice cream in the freezer and get started on dinner. Rachel pulled me down to her bunk and whispered, "Jane and I had a talk."

"A talk?"

"Yeah. I asked her if she has a thing for you."

"What? Why would you do that? What does that even mean?"

"It means that she likes you as more than a friend."

"What did she say?"

"She said, 'What if I do?' and I said it's okay with me as long as she's careful with you because you're my best friend."

I couldn't think what to say.

"Do you like her that way?"

"Did she ask you if I did?"

"Well, not exactly, but I could tell she wants to know. So do you?"

"I guess so. I mean, I know what I feel, but I thought that kind of thing was, I don't know, deviant or something. People get arrested for it, right? Like it's against the law. Girls are supposed to like boys."

"Maybe it's time to stop listening to what everyone says you're supposed to do, Cal. Maybe it's time to do what you think is right for you."

I looked at her pixie face, so cute and so serious at the same time.

"You are weirdly wise sometimes."

"You should always listen to me. And, by the way, I think Jane is A-Okay."

I pushed at Rachel playfully and laughed as we made our way to the kitchen. Then, glancing up to see Jane stirring pots of beans and potatoes, I suddenly felt shy, my face burning with embarrassment at what Rachel and I had been talking about.

"This gourmet meal is just about ready to serve," Jane said, smiling and winking at me.

As we sat slurping ice cream after dinner, we couldn't avoid the subject of our predicament any longer. I figured we were all thinking the same thing. Do we go to Tyler tomorrow, or do we go back home and forget this whole thing?

"We're tempting fate," Jane said. "But if you all are game, so am I."

"I don't know, y'all," I said. "This is super dangerous. And it doesn't have anything to do with either one of you. This is my problem."

"That's the dumbest thing I've ever heard," Rachel said. "We've been in this together since day one. We have to go where this takes us. Why did we even start if we didn't plan on finishing?"

I looked from Rachel to Jane and back again. If I was going, they were going with me.

"How far is it to Tyler?" I asked.

They smiled and we all high-fived.

Rachel drew KP duty and stayed downstairs to clean up. As Jane and I climbed the stairs, my brain flooded with crazy thoughts of getting close to her, of touching her, of kissing her.

"Are you okay?" she asked.

"Of course. Why not?"

"Rachel said something to me in the grocery store today."

I stopped, waiting for her to go on.

Jane hesitated. "She…I guess she thinks…that you and I—"

She looked at me expectantly, as though she thought I might fill in the blanks.

"You and I…?"

"You're going to make me say it."

"Tell me what you're talking about."

"She thinks you and I are more than just friends."

"Are we?"

"You need to stop teasing me. It's not fair."

That stung. I had to look away. I knew she was right. "I need time."

"Take all you need," she said and sprinted the rest of the way up to the bunk room.

Neither one of us said anything as we brushed our teeth and washed our faces. Rachel was too tired to notice.

"Lights out!" one of the supervisors called once we were all ready for bed.

In my bunk I was wide-awake. I looked over at Jane. She was asleep. I could hear her breathing, soft and steady. I slipped out of my bunk and climbed up to hers. I got under the sheet that lightly covered her, pushing her over as she woke up. She was wearing a short nightgown that felt silky. I had on a cotton T-shirt.

"Hey, you," she said.

"Do you mind me busting in on you?"

"I'm not gonna throw you out."

She was propped up on her elbow, looking at me in the dark. I pushed her onto her back. I wrapped myself around her and pressed my mouth to hers. She surprised me by opening it right away. Her tongue pressed through my lips and tickled the roof of my mouth. I laughed a little and she put her hands under my shirt. She moved slowly up my stomach to my chest, her fingers circling my nipples. Heat rushed from my head to between my legs. I couldn't stop a tiny sound from slipping out as I tried to breathe through the sensation that took over my body and mind.

I felt her hand between my legs, her fingers pressing against me. As she slipped inside me, the throbbing explosion blocked out everything else in the world. I reached for her and copied what she did, pressing my hand hard against her. When I hesitated to go further, she guided me, gasping into my ear as I made contact. We rocked against each other and shook the bunk so hard I thought the rest of the room would wake up. We held each other until we quieted. I fell asleep next to her.

"Time to get up," Jane whispered, gently shaking me early the next morning. Rachel was still asleep in her bunk. I felt terrified, thinking about what I'd done.

"It's okay," Jane mouthed, reading the look on my face.

Lucky for me, we had to get up and out right away. I did not want to think too much about how amazing last night had felt and how much I wanted to do it again.

CHAPTER TWENTY

We were on track to leave Ft. Worth before eight a.m. According to our calculations, it would take us about two and a half hours to get to Tyler. As we sat in a long line at the pumps, we discussed our plan, such as it was.

"Like I told y'all," Rachel said, "my uncle Dan used to work at that refinery. And my cousin Steve has worked there the last two summers. He's a senior now and he's a cool guy. Maybe he could give us some inside scoop on the lay of the land."

"Are you sure you can trust him?" I asked.

"Oh, yeah. Me and him are close. Whenever we have a family reunion, we're the ones in charge of all the cousins. I've had his back a million times. Like when he snuck his girlfriend into his tent this one time."

"Sounds like our best bet," Jane said. "How can you get in touch with him?"

"I know where his high school is. We can try to catch him at lunch."

The drive to Tyler was easy, but just as we got to the edge of town, I noticed we had been passed by at least three cars that looked like unmarked Texas Ranger cruisers.

"Am I imagining things, or does it seem like there's a bunch of Rangers coming into town?"

"I think you're right," Jane said. "Look, there's a Ranger patrol car coming up on us now."

"So they took our lead," I said, smirking.

"Hey, I'm going to try breaking into their frequency with my radio. I've been studying up on that," Rachel said.

"Since when?" I said.

"You don't know everything about me."

Rachel dug a radio out of her pack. She fiddled with it until she picked up a piece of conversation that sounded like them.

"Targets identified and moving toward rendezvous point," a male voice crackled.

"Team meeting at 1200 hours. Local PD HQ," said another voice.

I glanced at the other two, gulping. "They definitely think something is happening here."

The reality started to sink in. "I'm scared," I said. "I'm worried my mom is right in the middle of all this. What's going to happen to her?"

Rachel reached from the backseat to hug me. Jane squeezed my hand.

"We'll be right there with you. Whatever happens," Rachel said.

I took a deep breath and did my best to steady my thoughts. "Let's figure out where the police headquarters is. That's where the Rangers are meeting up. Maybe we can listen in on their briefing. At least get some idea what time they think this is going down."

We found the address for the police headquarters, but first we had to go to Steve's high school to see if we could catch him on lunch break.

"There's his car," Rachel said as we pulled into the parking lot. "Let's wait there. He probably goes off campus for lunch since he's a senior."

Sure enough, it hadn't been ten minutes before Rachel spotted him. She jumped out of the car and headed toward him, arms wide for a big hug. She jumped into his arms. Jane and I got out to introduce ourselves.

"What in the world," he said. "What are you doing here?"

When we told him all about it, he shook his head in disbelief. "I don't know, girls. This sounds kinda crazy. I guess I can help you, but are you sure you want to do this? All kinds of things could go wrong."

"That's true. But we've come this far. Look, we just want to get a bird's-eye view of what happens out there. I want to see for myself whether my mom is part of this or just being dragged along. Can you understand that?"

He looked at me, shuffling his feet. "I get it."

"So you'll help?" Rachel asked.

He nodded. "I know the place inside and out. Once you find out the details, let me know and I'll see what I can do."

Rachel gave him a hug and told him to be near the phone later.

"He's cool," I said as we got back in the car and headed toward the police station.

When we got there, sure enough, I counted eight Texas Ranger patrol cars outside the station, along with several unmarked cars that I had learned to recognize as law enforcement. We parked across the street at the opposite end of the block. There was no doubt in my mind they were here to bust the Brazos River Gang. Rachel switched on the radio to the channel she had found earlier. Nothing.

"They aren't broadcasting anything right now," she said.

"Yeah, 'cause they're all inside the station," I said. "We have to think of something else."

"Let's walk around the building," Jane said. "We might find a way to listen in."

The streets were quiet in this part of town, where there weren't any shops or cafés, so it seemed like no one would notice us. We strolled confidently, not rushing, up the street.

"Behind the building," Jane said, motioning us to follow.

"Look." Rachel pointed to a row of windows on the first floor. "I see them. They're all in that room."

We ducked down quickly, crawling along the ground under the windowsills. After eight or ten feet, we heard the sound of a man's voice. One of the windows must have been open. We kept going as the sound grew louder and then it was obvious which spot was the best. I listened as hard as I could, trying to catch every word.

Here's what I heard:

"Let's talk about the location and what we expect," said a booming authoritative voice. "Penco Oil Company is a local, family-owned business that has been here in Tyler since 1933. They have one location, on Palace Avenue. They started out as a Standard of Ohio oil and gas distributor and now they distribute for Shell Oil. A guy on the inside has admitted to us that he's been paid to look the other way while somebody steals smaller amounts of gasoline."

Bev added, "We expect the gang to arrive at the refinery after dark, most likely between seven and nine p.m. They will have about twenty minutes to extract as much gas as they can. That's how much time the inside guy will give them."

"Will we make the arrest tonight?" someone asked.

"If all goes well," Bev said.

"What about Joyce Long? Should we treat her as a hostage? Or a perpetrator?"

I caught my breath. Jane and Rachel grabbed for my hands.

"For our purposes tonight, we have to assume she is acting on her own accord. Treat her like everyone else, until there's a reason to believe differently."

I slumped to the ground, my heart beating against my chest so hard it hurt like someone was punching me.

"Everybody get some rest for the next couple of hours. We regroup here at five p.m. sharp," the booming male voice said.

"Let's get out of here," Jane said, pulling me up to all fours.

We scrambled back along the wall under the windows, through the alley, and back to the street. We emerged calmly, looking around to find the way clear. Back in the car, Jane drove us a few blocks away to a residential area where we slipped into an alley.

"How are you doing?" Rachel asked me.

I shrugged. "I don't know. I have a bad feeling about this. They're going to treat her like one of the gang, and, if things get violent…" I couldn't finish my thought. My mother could get killed and I knew it.

"I wonder if there's any way we could get to Joyce," Jane said.

"What do you mean?"

"Watch for the gang to arrive. Somehow get to her. Signal her."

I shook my head. "I don't think that makes sense. She's either with them voluntarily, in which case a signal wouldn't mean anything to her, or she's a hostage and they would have her tied up or something, where we couldn't get to her."

"I think we should try," Rachel said.

"Well, this all comes down to how Steve can help us. We need to figure out what he can do."

With that, we left the alley in search of a phone booth. Steve answered on the first ring. Rachel spoke to him for a couple of minutes before returning to the car to give us the scoop. He would meet us at Penco Oil in half an hour. He had an idea about where to set us up.

We stopped at a McDonald's drive-through for burgers and fries, but I didn't have much of an appetite.

"You need to eat," said Rachel. "Keep up your strength."

I forced the food down, but didn't feel well at all.

"You don't look so good," Jane said. "Maybe this is not such a good idea. We don't have to go through with it, you know."

I pulled myself together. "I'm fine. I just need to close my eyes for a few minutes. I'm not going to quit now. Let's go."

I leaned my head back on the seat and Jane drove toward Penco. It was on the outskirts of town in a remote industrial area with a few warehouses scattered here and there. The bland-looking concrete building was surrounded by a big concrete pad and fenced with metal barbed wire. Steve was waiting there when we arrived.

"Do y'all have canteens and binoculars?" he asked. We nodded and he said, "Bring 'em."

We packed them in a duffel bag that Rachel carried. Then Jane pulled the car around to an out-of-the-way spot and covered it with brush to hide the license plate. Steve took us into the office up front and introduced us to Janine, the woman at the desk, explaining that we were in town on a school band trip. He told her he wanted to show us around. It was easy.

"We'll leave by the back way," Steve told her. "So, see you next time."

"Y'all have fun, honey," Janine said.

He waved and said hello to the guys we saw working in the building, saying, "just showing them around," as we passed by. We stopped by a water fountain to fill our canteens.

"You'll need water while you wait for all of this to go down."

We understood when we saw where he was going to put us. He showed us rafters at the top of the warehouse, probably thirty feet up.

"How do we get up there?"

"I'm gonna show you," he said, and walked us to what turned out to be a false wall. There were ladder steps inside the wall that went all the way to the roofline.

"There's a small platform up there. Just enough room for the three of you."

I felt a little queasy as I looked up to the top of the narrow ladder.

"I'll give the go-ahead when I'm sure no one will see you climbing," he said. "Then you're just gonna have to stay there and wait."

When we were safely up on the platform, we gave Steve the thumbs-up and off he went.

CHAPTER TWENTY-ONE

The sun went down and the dim lights of the refinery shed a pale yellow glow over the tanks and equipment below. Rachel turned on her radio in case she was able to pick up anything from the Rangers. Jane stood and looked outside through a gap between the top of the wall and the slant of the roof.

"This is a pretty good view. I can see quite a ways down the highway."

"Are the Rangers hiding out there somewhere?" Rachel asked.

"I guess so. They must be in the woods over there," Jane said from her perch. "There's a gully or ravine that disappears behind a long line of big old oak trees. About a hundred yards away."

"What time is it?" I asked.

"Six thirty," Jane said. "Hey, I think I see something."

Just then Rachel's radio crackled. "Suspects spotted."

"This is it," I said, taking a swallow from my canteen.

"Hand me my binoculars," Jane said.

"Here go you," I said. "What do you see now?"

"A van, a tanker—small one—and a pickup truck."

The radio crackled again. "Confirmed, tanker approaching. Stand by."

"They're almost here," Jane said. "Five minutes tops before they're in the parking lot."

"Turn the radio way down," I said. "We can't let them hear anything from up here."

I got my binoculars ready. I wanted to get a good look at them once they came inside.

"Turning into the parking lot. I'll lose sight of them now because of the angle," Jane said, jumping down off the ledge to join us on the platform.

The three of us trained our binoculars on the huge overhead door that would be opening to let them in. It felt like hours to me, but only minutes went by before the door came up.

"Joyce," Rachel said. "She's in the pickup. On the passenger side."

Several men got out of the van to help maneuver the tanker into the bay. Once it was in place, one of them took an oversized wrench from the pickup and worked on the valve on the vat of gasoline that was their target.

"Theft in progress," said someone on the radio.

"Move in," Bev said.

I kept my binoculars on Mom. Her face was passive. No expression. I couldn't tell if she was a part of this or not. Meanwhile, Jane was back up on her perch, watching for the Rangers.

"They're coming," she said.

"I hope they can do this without firing any shots," I said.

"I don't know," Jane said. "They're bringing an awful lot of firepower."

Just then, a loud pop went off and everyone on the floor below grabbed for their guns and ran toward the outside. I saw Mom get out of the pickup. Then I saw Hank pushing her out of the way, like he was telling her to go for cover. Without thinking, I moved to the edge of the platform and scaled down the ladder as fast as I could. Jane grabbed at me, but I ignored her. When I got to the floor, I scanned the room for any sign of Mom.

I spotted her, huddled behind a forklift and some other equipment.

"Mom," I said. "C'mon, I can get you out of here."

"What on earth," she shouted. "What are you doing here?"

"It doesn't matter," I said. "You can get away. I can save you."

"Cal, get out of here. You have no idea what you're doing. And I don't need to be saved."

"What?"

"Go," she said, scowling at me.

At that moment, Hank grabbed her hand and said, "Let's go." He looked at me with what seemed to me like a mixture of surprise and admiration. He nodded and then they were gone. I ran to the bay door and watched the van speed away as the Rangers got too slow a start. The pickup and the tanker sat abandoned.

I had no time to think about what my mother had just done because, when I looked back toward the ladder wall, I saw Jane frantically calling me over. I ran to her and saw Rachel crumpled on the ground.

"She fell from halfway up," Jane said, a look of terror on her face.

"Oh my god," I said, kneeling down beside her. "Rachel?"

She moaned but didn't move.

"I don't think we should touch her," Jane said. "I'm afraid she's got multiple broken bones and she might be bleeding inside."

"Where's her radio. We need to get help fast."

We found the radio in the duffel bag and just started screaming into it, asking for help from anyone who could hear us. Bev's voice interrupted us.

"Cal, is that you?"

"Yes, please, we need help. We're inside the building. Rachel's hurt." I was screaming and crying frantically, scared my best friend was dying at my feet.

Bev came within a few minutes, a medical team following close behind. They were very careful putting Rachel on a stretcher. She whimpered weakly but didn't open her eyes. I tried to get close to her, but the medic stopped me.

"Will she be okay?"

"We'll do our best," he said. "The faster we get her to the hospital, the better."

"Can we go with her?" Jane asked.

"Not enough room," he said as the stretcher moved quickly to their van.

We stood watching in silence as the medical team sped off down the highway. I collapsed into Jane's arms, sobbing.

"I'll never forgive myself for this! Never!"

Jane held me tight, tears covering her face too. "She'll be okay," Jane said over and over, trying to convince us both. "She has to be."

"Stay here," Bev said to us sternly. "I'll be back."

We sat on the floor for almost an hour before she finally came back.

"I know you're probably going to arrest us," I said, "but can we find out how Rachel is doing?"

Bev looked at us with a mixture of anger and sympathy.

"They got her stabilized at the hospital in Tyler," she said, "but they are waiting for a critical care ambulance to take her to Dallas."

"Oh my god," I said. "I have to see her."

"No," Bev said. "You need to start acting like who you are, which is a fifteen-year-old girl who should be home and in school. It's going to take every trick in my book to keep you out of the juvenile justice system."

I stared at the ground, unable to look her in the eye. Jane reached for my hand and we huddled together, waiting for what would happen next.

"Can we at least know what happened out there?" Jane asked. "With the gang and with Cal's mom?"

Bev sighed, as if considering what to tell us, if anything.

"The bottom line is they got away. There was a mistake by the Tyler police that gave them an opening. So we're back to square one."

"I spoke to my mom," I said sheepishly.

"What?"

"Yeah, I got close enough. She told me to get away. That she didn't need to be saved from anything."

"What was your sense of her situation? Was she acting on her own free will?"

I shrugged. "I couldn't tell. That guy, Hank Hart, he came and pulled her away. Maybe he was forcing her to go along? I just don't know."

"You'll let me know if she contacts you?"

"Do you think she will?"

"There's no way to predict, but sure, she might."

"What are you going to do with us?" Jane asked.

"We're keeping you overnight at a motel in town. Then, assuming I can work it out with my superiors, we're sending you home tomorrow."

"Home?" I asked. "By myself?"

"Home to your dad's," Bev said.

I didn't even try to argue with her. I knew I'd be stuck at my dad's until further notice. Bev motioned to some Rangers standing nearby and they helped us gather up our things and escorted us to a van outside.

"They will get you checked into your room," Bev said. "Stay there. I'll be next door."

I was out of my mind, thinking about everything that just happened, knowing I was responsible for Rachel getting hurt. And then, on top of it, being sent home. Jane and I sat in the back of the van, helpless.

"It's my fault," I said.

"It's not your fault."

"I never should have involved either one of you in this."

"Cal, we came on our own. Because we wanted to. Because we're a team."

"Thank you," I said. "I really love you. As a friend, I mean."

"Silly girl," Jane whispered. "What else would I be but a friend?"

We rode the rest of the way in silence.

Early the next morning, the telephone rang. I looked at the clock, groggy and cloudy-eyed. It was six a.m.

"Please come down to the lobby with your bags packed," said a male voice.

"What? Where's Bev—"

"Now, please," said the voice, sternly.

I woke Jane up and told her what the voice had said.

"C'mon," I said, "we better get moving."

Bev was not there when we got down to the lobby. In fact, none of the Texas Rangers were there. It was only the Tyler police.

"Outside. There's a truck waiting," said a sergeant, pointing to a vehicle parked in front of the entrance.

"What's happening? What about my car?" Jane asked, stepping toward him.

"Your car's impounded. You're getting a ride to Dallas. Someone's meeting you there."

"Who?" I asked.

"The Rangers didn't disclose that to us. But they'll have paperwork."

Jane and I looked at each other. I felt like a prisoner who was being hauled off to jail. "Can I make a phone call?"

"I can't authorize long distance," he said.

"I'll call collect."

He waved me over to the girl at the motel desk. She helped me make the call.

"Grandma," I said after the collect call was accepted. "Jane and I are being shipped back to—"

"I know," Grandma interrupted. "Your dad's the one meeting you."

"But Grandma!"

"There's nothin' I can do about it," she said. "Wish I could, but he's hoppin' mad."

"Did you hear what happened to Rachel?"

"Oh, yes ma'am, I did. And it's all over the news now."

"Oh, no. What are they saying? Is she okay?"

"It's not good, but they think—"

The sergeant took the telephone out of my hand.

"Hey!"

"Time to go," he said, nodding toward the waiting truck.

Men on both sides took our arms and escorted us quickly through the doors and into the police vehicle.

"Look," Jane said, pointing to photographers snapping our pictures as they shoved us into the backseat.

At this point, we started to realize how serious—and public— our situation was and how stupid we had been to think we could control anything. The truck sped away, almost running over one of the photographers and throwing us to the floorboard.

"Hey," I yelled out to the driver. "Take it easy!"

"Shut your trap!" he yelled back at us.

As we rolled along the highway at eighty-five miles an hour, a horrible scene played out in my mind. My life was breaking apart in front of me. I saw my house split up and pieces flying in all different directions. I suddenly had the sensation of floating away into space, disconnected from everything I'd even known. I started hyperventilating.

"What's wrong?" Jane said, grabbing my hand. "You need to calm down."

She shook me and I came back to Earth.

"You were breathing so hard and fast. I thought you were going to pass out."

I looked at her, but I couldn't speak. It felt like someone had poured gravel down my throat or stuffed it with cotton.

"Cal!" Jane took me by the shoulders and stared into my eyes like she couldn't find me in there.

I gasped out a few words, "Okay…I will be…okay."

She hugged me tightly, stroking my hair and saying over and over, "I'm here. I'll take care of you."

When we got to Dallas two hours later, I spotted my father standing outside his car talking to two Texas Rangers. As we pulled up next to the patrol car, I saw Jane's father walking out of the state highway building nearby.

"Your dad," I said, gripping Jane's arm.

"That's not good," Jane said. "They weren't supposed to be home from their East Coast trip yet."

"Well, girls, it's quite the adventure you've been on," Jane's father said ruefully as we got out of the truck.

"Let's go," Dad said, picking up my suitcase and opening his car door.

"Jane," I said, in a panic, suddenly realizing we were being separated on the spot.

"You've spent enough time together," Dad said. "In the car," he said, daring me to challenge him.

As we drove away, I looked back, trying to keep Jane in my sight as long as possible. Her father was dragging her toward his car as she held both arms out in my direction. Tears streamed down my face and I held my hand to the window, imagining that I was touching Jane's.

CHAPTER TWENTY-TWO

What a weird feeling it was to go back to school a few days later. The thought of it was silly to me. With my mother still missing, Rachel in the hospital fighting for her life, and Jane and I separated, the idea of sitting in a classroom was trivial.

Every night at my dad's had been a sleepless one, and not just because the bed in his apartment was saggy and uncomfortable. Being at his house was like being in a straightjacket. I felt trapped. I even imagined I couldn't catch my breath sometimes. I started to think I might be going a little crazy.

I got up at sunrise on my first day back at school. "This stinks," I mumbled, throwing off the covers.

I looked out the dingy window of my tiny room, which was really his office. The sight made me feel even worse. Dirty pickup trucks and broken down beat-up old cars lined the parking lot below. It looked like a used car lot. I got dressed and went into the kitchen, looking for cereal, but couldn't find any. Dad walked in.

"There's no Cheerios," I said.

He tossed the morning newspaper on the kitchen table and opened the refrigerator door.

"There's eggs," he said. "And some bacon. Fry us up some."

I gave him a blank look.

"Don't you know how to cook?"

I turned and started to leave the room.

"Hey!" he said. "I'm talking to you."

"I hate this," I said, slumping into a chair.

"I don't know what you think you're gonna do," he said, crossing his arms and leaning back on two legs of the chair.

"I can tell you what I'm not gonna do," I said, crossing my arms too. "I'm not gonna cook for you."

"Fine," he said, getting up and opening the refrigerator. "I'll make it myself. You need to eat something and then we gotta get you to school."

I watched him cooking, thinking maybe I was being too hard on him. After all, he hadn't really done anything. It wasn't his fault my mother had gone crazy. I offered to set the table. We ate in silence and quickly cleaned up together. As we drove to school, I fidgeted with my book bag.

"I want to see Rachel."

"She's still in Dallas."

"She's probably gonna be there for a long time," I said. "I want to see her."

He strummed the steering wheel, letting out a long sigh. "I'll talk to her dad. See what the visitor rules are."

When I got to school, the first thing I did was look for Jane. We hadn't been allowed to speak to each other since we were separated in Dallas. Dad had forbidden me to use the telephone, and he told Jane to stop calling after she'd tried to reach me several times.

I ran up the stairs to the junior hall. I knew she had calculus first period, so I walked in that direction. I didn't see her. I stopped a girl I knew on the way in.

"Have you seen Jane Rawlings?" I asked.

"They said she's not coming back," the girl said.

"What are you talking about?"

"She's in my homeroom, well, she was supposed to be. Her parents sent her to boarding school."

A wave of nausea washed over me and my head felt like it was floating off my body. I grabbed onto the doorjamb to steady myself. I couldn't think.

"Are you okay?" the girl asked.

"Sorry," I said and stumbled down the hall. I saw the principal coming toward me and dashed into the girls' restroom.

"Cal," he called from the hallway. "What's wrong? You need to get to class."

"I'm coming," I said, splashing water on my face and trying to calm down.

The rest of the day, I felt like I was in a pool up to my neck, treading water and going under every so often. Kids tried to talk to me and find out what happened in Palo Duro Canyon and Tyler. I gave them answers, but it didn't seem like me talking. There was a soupy fog in my head that filtered everything coming into my ears and slowed my responses to half speed.

Somehow, I made it to the end of the day. When I got home to find Dad home too, I was struck by how small the place was. I closed myself in the bathroom, sat on the toilet seat and stared straight ahead, using every ounce of willpower to stop myself from screaming.

Not knowing where they had sent Jane or when I would see her again hit me almost as hard as Rachel being in the hospital. And realizing that I was to blame, at least in part, for the situation both of them were in, made me ache inside. Soon the rock-hard plastic toilet seat became too uncomfortable to bear. I stood up, rubbing my butt and thinking, *one step at a time*. That's how we got through things. I would see Rachel. I would find Jane. My mother would return. Everything would be okay.

I finally left the bathroom and went straight to Dad's office, telling him I wasn't hungry for dinner. I sat on the bed, staring at the bookcase. When I saw his copy of the Bible on the shelf, I reached for it almost without thinking. There was a time when I got something out of reading it. Maybe it would help. I opened it at the ribbon marker—the Twenty-third Psalm. I read the last part of it out loud. "Yea, though I walk through the valley of the shadow of death, I shall fear no evil, for thou art with me; thy rod and thy staff, they comfort me. Thou preparest a table before me in the presence of mine enemies: Thou has anointed my head with oil; my cup runneth over. Surely goodness and mercy shall follow me all the days of my life; And I shall dwell in the House of the Lord forever."

I felt a little calmer after reading those words, somehow confident that I would find a way to put my life back in order. I fell asleep thinking about Jane in the bunk at the YWCA in Ft. Worth. And I didn't feel guilty at all.

The next morning, desperate to be alone, I decided to walk to school instead of riding with Dad. The walk was a blissful half hour. The sunrise was just beginning to warm the earth and there was a gentle breeze in the air. I walked by someone cutting their grass and the smell of the freshly mowed lawn comforted me. I stopped for a second or two to enjoy the peace.

As I approached the high school parking lot, a pickup truck slowed beside me. I looked up at the driver, a man wearing a cowboy hat and dark glasses. I recognized him as one of the Hart boys. I stopped short, looking left and right for an escape route. He reached out of the window with a small white envelope in his hand. It took me a few seconds to realize he was handing it to me. I grabbed it and he sped away.

There was a card inside. It was a greeting card with cute little children drawn on the front and a handwritten note on the inside. I recognized the handwriting immediately as my mother's. My racing heart made my fingers tremble as I held it up to read. *Cal, I need to see you. Please meet me after school today at the Daisy Diner across from the entrance to City Park. Love, Mom.*

Shaking, I stuffed the card into my book bag, looking around to see if anyone was watching. Nobody was paying attention to me.

I spent the day distracted, unable to focus on anything in the classroom, thinking about the note. I wasn't sure I should go, or if I even wanted to go. I was desperate to talk it over with someone—Jane, Rachel, or Grandma. Of course, I couldn't talk to any of them. I was alone. Finally, during study hall, I decided to make a collect call to Grandma. I had to convince the student monitor to let me go, promising him the inside scoop on how Rachel got hurt.

I went to the school office and begged to use a telephone in one of the unoccupied rooms. But just as I was about to dial, I had second thoughts. Maybe I shouldn't involve Grandma in this. I didn't know where it was going and I didn't want her to get caught up in something that could land her in jail. Once I met with Mom, if I did, I would be compromised. Anything I found out I would be obligated to turn over to the Texas Rangers. But this was my mother and I wasn't sure that was what I would do. It was all speculation for now, but why mix Grandma into the mess at this point? I decided I would meet Mom—alone.

I approached the diner, scared out of my wits, looking over my shoulder as I opened the door. I glanced around quickly but didn't see Mom. The lady at the hostess stand asked me if I wanted to sit down.

"Okay," I said. "I'm waiting for someone."

"Here you go, hon," she said. "I'll put you in the window so you can watch for your friend."

I sat down on the tufted red leather bench seat, nervously watching the front door, cigarette smoke from the booth behind me enveloping me in an eerie gray cloud. I ordered a Coke when the waitress came by. I looked at my watch. It was almost four o'clock.

"Hey, there," said Mom, appearing out of nowhere and scooting into the bench across from me. She wore a disguise that made her look much older, more like a grandmother.

"Where did you come from?"

"I snuck in through the kitchen. These folks are friends."

"The diner people are in on this?"

She ignored that question. I stared at her, trying to recognize any resemblance to the woman I knew as my mother. It wasn't just the disguise. It was everything about her. She gave off an energy I had never felt from her before. I couldn't think of anything more to say.

"Are you doing okay?" she asked.

"No," I said. "Are you kidding me?"

She reached across the table, trying to touch me, but I pushed away from her. "I understand, but—"

"I don't think you do," I hissed. "Rachel almost died."

She sat back, taking a deep breath. I thought I caught a flicker of a smile playing across her face. "Well, darlin', I think that's on you," she said, folding her arms.

It was unbelievable. She couldn't care less about Rachel. *Who is this woman?*

I looked at her through slits as fierce as I could make them, gritting my teeth, "What do you want?"

She took a pack of Newports out of her purse and lit one. "I need your help with something," she said.

I gripped the Coke in front of me even tighter. I didn't say anything. She flicked her cigarette into the ashtray.

"You know about Hank."

I sipped the Coke and slightly nodded.

"Whatever you've heard, it's only half the truth."

"Mom, you're part of a crime ring. What are you doing?"

"Here's the bottom line," she said, leaning over the linoleum table. "If I can get them a piece of information they want, they'll let me go. I can come home."

I banged my hand on the table. "Why don't you go to the police? Turn yourself in?"

She shifted, shaking her head. "This is serious business, Cal. They're watching my every move. If I go to the police, I'm dead."

"How did this happen? It's because of him, isn't it?"

She shouted over her shoulder to the waitress, "Jenny! Bring me a shot a Jim Beam."

"All of a sudden you drink?" I said as the waitress slid the bourbon across the table.

"Here's what I need from you," she said, throwing back the shot. "Your dad has a logbook for work—"

"Oh, no," I said. I was ready to leave.

"Just wait," she said. She grabbed my hand and pulled me back. "All I need is the date and time of the next big refinery shipment out of Amarillo."

"Mom!" I tried to pull away.

"I have a week," she said, tears brimming over her eyelashes. "Please help me get out of this mess."

I stopped resisting and looked into her eyes, wanting to believe her.

"Here's how to reach me."

She handed me a crumpled piece of paper and hurried out of the diner the way she came in. I stood there stunned, watching her go.

"Don't worry about the check, honey," the waitress said, clearing the table.

I left the diner in a daze, walking aimlessly until I ended up at my mom's house. I stared across at Rachel's, filled with misery and regret, and cried bitter tears. The more I thought about it, the more I worried my mother was not an innocent bystander in this whole convoluted series of events. But yet, I still wanted to believe she could be saved, even if she had been romanced into crime by that evil man. As I headed to my dad's, I knew I would do what she had asked.

CHAPTER TWENTY-THREE

I was crossed-legged on my bed in the dark when Dad got home that night. I hadn't bothered to get up to turn on the light when the sun went down. I had been sitting there for a couple of hours, staring at the wall, my body feeling like it weighed a thousand pounds and I'd never be able to move again. I couldn't help thinking that I had somehow brought this all on myself. What I had done with Jane was wrong and I didn't even regret it.

God was punishing me for my sins with Jane. I deserved it. You can't fall in love with someone of the same sex. Everything they preach from the pulpit tells you that you can't get away with things like that. How did I think I could escape the consequences? God had separated me from Jane and had taken away my best friend. All because I was...I couldn't even say the word to myself.

Dad called me from the other room and I forced myself to get up.

"Rachel's been asking to see you," he said, hanging up the telephone.

"Really?"

"That was Rachel's dad. She's doing better and she really wants you to visit, so I said I'd bring you down. We'll leave first thing in the morning."

"Thank you, Dad, really. I know it's not easy for you to just take off."

I watched him putting his work things away in the closet. He always carried a small leather portfolio that zipped up like a pouch. I thought about Mom's reference to the logbook and rubbed my eyes with a sigh.

"Something wrong?" he asked.

"No, no, I'm just thinking about what to bring Rachel. Could we stop at Stuckey's on the way? She loves those disgusting pecan logs."

"That's easy enough," he said.

When the apartment was still and Dad was asleep, I went into the living room as quietly as I could and opened the hall closet. I used a flashlight to find the leather portfolio. My heart pounded in my ears as I unzipped it and looked inside. I found a small notebook and saw what appeared to be a schedule of places, dates, and times. It didn't say what the schedule was for, but I assumed it was about the refinery shipments. Flipping through it, I saw notes about deliveries to Amarillo later that month.

This must be what she's looking for. I memorized the information and put the notebook and the portfolio back in its place. I wasn't sure I would go through with it. I didn't owe her anything. On the other hand, if this was all she needed to get away from them... My head hurt. I couldn't think about it anymore.

Dad and I left early the next morning, Saturday, making the three-hundred-mile trip in less than six hours. We only stopped once to get Rachel's pecan log. I wanted to avoid talking, so I pretended to sleep for most of the drive, listening to the stereo playing the collection of eight tracks Dad had in the car. But as we got closer to Dallas, he insisted on bringing up the subject of my mother.

"I know you thought you were helping her with that escapade in the canyon." I didn't say anything. "But that's when they figured out she's part of this thing." He looked at me for a reaction, but I didn't look back. "She's a criminal, Cal."

"I know that's how it looks," I said.

"That's how it is," he said. "And it's not going to end well."

I stared straight ahead for the rest of the ride. He stayed quiet too. He knew I wasn't going to say anything else.

Once we arrived at the hospital, I spotted Rachel's mom and ran into her arms. I cried and cried, unable to stop. She held me while I heaved and wailed, overcome with grief I hadn't realized was trapped inside.

"She's gonna be okay, sweetie," she said. "She can't wait to see you."

Standing at the door of her room, I felt so messed up, almost afraid now to go inside. When I saw her, I couldn't believe how pale and frail she looked. I guess the shock on my face showed.

"Not my best look, huh?" she said with a laugh.

"You scared me."

She reached for my hand. "How are you?"

I sat on the bed next to her. "Missing you. And Jane."

"What happened to Jane?"

Now the tears were coming back. "Her parents sent her away. She's at boarding school. I'm not even sure where. I think it's in New York."

"Oh, Cal, that's terrible. You haven't even talked to her?"

I shook my head. I took a tissue from the box next to Rachel's bed, wiped my face, and blew my nose. "I had a meeting with my mom."

"How?"

"The gang arranged it. She says they'll let her go if she gets them information on refinery deliveries just one more time."

"And she needs you for that?"

"Yeah, I stole it from my dad's notebook last night."

"How do you know they'll let her go?"

"I don't. But what if I don't help her and something terrible happens?"

"How much time do you have?"

"Mom said she had a week. That was yesterday."

"I don't know, Cal. I hate to say this, but what if she's lying?"

"I just can't believe she would do that to me," I said through tears again.

"I'm sorry," Rachel said. "I didn't mean—"

"No, it's okay. I'd feel the same way if it was the other way around."

"Just be careful. If you do it, you're part of the crime."

"Don't you think this is almost like self-defense?" I said. I was up, pacing the room. "I'm only doing it to save her."

"I guess you could argue that, but I don't know."

"My dad says she's straight-up a criminal."

"Really? No room for doubt?"

"Not a bit. He says it won't end well."

Rachel nodded and leaned back on her pillow, closing her eyes. "I think you should listen to him."

"You look tired," I said. "Maybe you should take a nap. I'll go down to the cafeteria and wait for Dad."

"Okay," Rachel said. "Cal? Don't give up on Jane."

"Are you sure? Sometimes I think that…how I feel about her is, you know, why all this other bad stuff is happening."

"Stop it. Don't think that way. You're the best person I know. Whatever you have going with Jane can't be a sin."

I kissed her on the forehead as she fell asleep, and then I crept quietly out of the room.

I bought a Dr. Pepper in the cafeteria and thought about how I could get in touch with Jane. I knew she must be trying to call or send letters, but my dad was blocking communication. The mail came to a locked mailbox in the parking lot of the apartment building and he had the only key. By the time he came back for me, I had made up my mind to pay a visit to

Jane's parents and persuade them to give me Jane's address and a telephone number. I would ride my bike over there as soon as I got back to town. Rachel was right. I would never give up on Jane, no matter what anyone, including God, had to say about it.

CHAPTER TWENTY-FOUR

When Dad and I got back home the next afternoon, I made an excuse to him, grabbed my bike and rode straight to Jane's parents' place. I parked near the garage and ran to the front door, pushing the chime.

Jane's brother, Ted, opened the door.

"Ted!" I stepped inside before he could decide not to let me in.

"Well, hello," he said. "Come on in."

"You have to help me get in touch with Jane."

"Hold on a minute," he said. "Let's go to the kitchen."

I followed him and sat on one of the barstools at the counter while he opened the refrigerator and pulled out a milk carton.

"Want some?"

"No, thanks," I said, impatient to get to the point. "I don't mean to be rude. It's just that I really want to talk to Jane. And I have no idea where she is."

"Well," he said. "I could tell you, but if my parents find out, they'll be furious."

"But why? Why would they care if I talk to her?"

He drained his glass of milk before responding. "It's kind of an intervention."

"What does that mean?"

"You know, breaking you up."

I felt red-hot and looked away.

"They... Well, really it's Mom... She thinks you two are... you know, lez."

I stared at the counter in front of me, humiliated. "Could I have some water?"

He took a glass from the cabinet and filled it from a pitcher in the refrigerator. I took a drink and felt the cold water trace my throat down into my stomach. "Will you help me or not?"

He took a slip of paper and wrote something on it. "I didn't give this to you. Understood?"

I nodded and stormed out of the house, furious that her parents would do this to us. I punched the garage door, trying to knock a hole in it. I drew back a bloody fist and thought I might have broken my hand. "Crap!"

I got on my bike and rode blindly as fast as I could, paying no attention to where I was going. A few blocks away, I stopped the bike, laid it down and sat on the curb. I was almost delirious—from the travel, from thinking about Mom, from what Ted had told me. I had to force myself to focus on what I'd set out to do—get in touch with Jane. I pulled out the piece of paper Ted had handed me: *Jolsen Maynard School.*

I checked my watch to see if I still had time to get to the public library before it closed. "If I hurry."

At the library, I asked the librarian if there were books I could use to research boarding schools in the East. The librarian looked at me peculiarly, but she took me to a stack in the education section. She pulled down a book called *College Prep for Girls—Boarding Academies.*

I found a description of Jolsen Maynard School. "Founded in 1814, Jolsen Maynard School is a boarding academy for girls grades 9-12. Set on 137 beautiful acres in Syracuse, New York, Jolsen Maynard provides a unique educational setting for intellectually curious girls who want to explore the full range of engagement with their world."

There was a telephone number. I wrote it down. I wondered how I would get through to Jane if the school knew there was this girl in Texas who Jane's parents were trying to keep her away from. I would have to come up with a clever plan to get around that.

The next morning, Dad banged on my door, yelling at me to wake up. "You're gonna be late!"

I had overslept. I was still in my clothes from the night before. I'd fallen asleep dreaming a crazy mix-up of rescuing Jane from boarding school and bringing the Brazos River Gang to justice.

"Just give me a few minutes," I said.

Pull yourself together. Just take one thing at a time. I organized my schoolbooks and put them into the bag. I looked again at the number for the Jolsen Maynard School, and I tucked the small piece of paper into the back of my wallet.

On my way into the school building, I slipped around the side to the mechanical annex where Mom had told me to leave a date and time for another meeting at the diner. I tucked an envelope under the boiler—where her note had said to put it. It said I would meet her at the diner the next morning at seven a.m. I still wasn't sure if I was going to give her the information she'd asked for. It was going to come down to whether she could convince me that Dad was wrong about her.

In the meantime, I was just happy to be in class, acting as though I was a normal teenage girl. At the end of the day, I walked as fast as I could back to Dad's apartment. All I wanted was to talk to Jane and I had to come up with a plan. When I walked into the apartment, I was surprised to find Grandma there.

"Grandma!"

"Surprise! I couldn't stand it anymore. I had to see you."

"Oh my gosh, Grandma. You won't believe what all has gone on."

"Any news from your mom?"

I felt a twinge of guilt for not telling her about Mom. But I knew I had made the right decision. It was better for Grandma if she didn't know about all that. "Nothing yet."

"I heard you saw Rachel."

"Thank God she's okay. I was so scared."

"What about Jane?"

I dropped into a chair at the table. "She's at boarding school. In New York."

"What?"

"Can you believe it? Her parents sent her there just to keep us apart."

"Oh, honey, that's a shame. What is wrong with them?"

"Her mom is a monster."

"Now, now. I'm sure she thinks she's doing the right thing."

I pouted for a few seconds, but then had a brilliant idea. "Grandma, you could help me!"

"Anything, honey."

"I have the phone number of the school, but they aren't going to let me talk to her."

"Well, of course not. You're the problem, obviously."

We grinned at each other. "But you could pretend to be her aunt or something, get her on the phone and then I could talk to her. What do you think?"

Grandma rubbed her hands together. "I like it. Where's the number?"

I listened as Grandma used her Texas charm and pretended to be Jane's aunt, checking on her favorite niece. I wondered if Jane would figure it out before she answered the call.

"Hello, Jane, it's Bert," she said when Jane came on the line. "Here's Cal."

"You are so ingenious," Jane said.

"Not ingenious enough. You're the one in the fancy boarding school."

"I miss you."

"I miss you too. It looks nice. I read about it and saw pictures."

"It's okay. It's just, you know, the reason I'm here. That's the hard part."

"What did they say, your parents?"

"It doesn't matter."

"But do you think...do you think we are what they say?"

"I don't think we have to call it something, like it's a disease. I just feel the way I feel."

I pulled the phone as far as I could into the pantry where I had a little more privacy. "Tell me how you feel."

"You know I'm in a hallway."

I could feel her smiling. "You can do it."

"You make me so freaking hot. When I think about you, I can't see straight. Send me something—a T-shirt, anything, that you've been wearing."

"What will you do with it?"

"I'll put it on a pillow and sleep on it," she said, giggling.

"Oh my gosh!"

"Hey," Jane said, "how's everything else?"

"Weird. I need your advice."

"I don't know," Jane said after I told her what was going on. "You'll be conspiring with them if you do it. And there's no guarantee they'll let her go. What will you do if they don't?"

"I can't think that far ahead."

"Don't be a hero, Cal."

"What do you mean?"

"Even if you decide she's the victim, just give her the information and get away as fast as you can. Let her save herself."

I was quiet, thinking that over, not sure I wanted to commit.

"I mean it, Cal."

"Okay," I said, finally. "I get it."

"Let's set a time to talk again," she said. "I'll call you in forty-eight hours."

"Okay. Between four and five o'clock. I'll be by the phone."

When I hung up, Grandma gave me a snarly look with her arms crossed. "What was that I heard?"

"Grandma, I don't have a choice."

"You could go to the police."

"Mom says they'll kill her if we go to the police."

"Your mom says a lot of things. Why not call that nice Texas Ranger lady?"

"Please, just trust me. I can do this."

"Honey, I know you can do it. I just hope your momma doesn't disappoint you one more time."

The next morning on my way to meet Mom, I dropped a T-shirt in the mail to Jane. As I approached the diner, my nerves got the best of me. Butterflies flew up and down my insides. Once more I rehearsed what I planned to say to her. Then I closed my eyes for a second, took a deep breath, and opened the door.

When I stepped inside, someone immediately stepped behind me and locked the door. I looked around. One of the Hart brothers each stood in a corner of the room, guns stuck in their belts. I couldn't believe it. "What's going on? Where's my mother?"

Just then she walked out of the kitchen and into the room, this time not dressed in a disguise. Her shoulder-length frosted hair looked almost blond. She wore a miniskirt and black knee-high boots over fishnets.

"What the hell?" I said. "What's all this?" And then I realized the Hart boys worked for her. *Dad was right.*

"It's just a precaution, honey."

"Mom!"

"It's not that we don't trust you, sweetie, but there's a lot at stake here. Now, come with us."

"Wait, Mom, please. I don't want to go anywhere!"

"You don't have a choice," she said. "Go ahead," she told the one I knew was Warren.

He took my hands and tied them behind my back and then tried to put a blindfold around my eyes. "Stop! Mom! Don't do this to me!" I started screaming and crying and pulling away as hard as I could.

"Stay quiet or we'll have to put a gag in your mouth," she said over her shoulder as she headed into the kitchen. "But I'd rather not."

"I was trying to save you," I said, tears forming at the corners of my eyes.

She walked away from me and hesitated for just half a step, then kept walking, saying nothing. I struggled against the man who pressed a blindfold over my eyes and forced me out the back and into a vehicle that must have been a truck. Crowded between two of the large Hart brothers, I felt frighteningly alone. And desperate. Dread came over me like a suffocating pair of hands at my throat. I couldn't think. I had no idea what to do or how I would get out of this trap.

CHAPTER TWENTY-FIVE

When I finally found my voice, I shouted, "Where are we going?"

No one responded.

"Please, where are you taking me?"

Still no one responded. I slumped back against the seat, growing angrier, trying to think. I don't know how this came into my head, but I started singing. "Amazing Grace, how sweet the sound, that saved a wretch like me. I once was lost, but now I'm found. Was blind, but now I see."

"Shut up!"

I recognized Warren's voice. *At least I got a rise out of him.*

I estimated it was about forty-five minutes before we stopped and they took me out of the truck and into a building where they removed the blindfold and the rope from my wrists. I looked around and saw what appeared to be a combination of a garage and a warehouse. It was so hot in there it felt like the air weighed a thousand pounds, and I could hardly catch my breath. There were no windows and the doors were solid metal, so I couldn't tell anything about exactly where they had taken me. I saw tanker trucks parked inside the building, along with several desks and some couches and soft chairs.

Someone offered me a sandwich and a Coke.

"Do you have Dr. Pepper?" I asked.

He pointed to a small refrigerator and I opened it, finding several bottles of it inside. I sat on one of the couches eating the sandwich, waiting for something to happen. Sweat rolled down my back. Before too long, my mother walked in through the main door of the building. She came straight to me and stood over me, taking her finger and lifting my face to look at her.

"I'm sure you think I'm being a little rough on you," she said.

"I'm okay," I said, batting her hand away.

"I know you're wondering why you're here."

She sat down on the couch opposite me.

"I did what you asked me to do. I have the information," I said, slamming my drink bottle down on the coffee table between us.

"I wanted to test you."

"Test me?"

"I wanted to see how good you are."

"Do you really think you can recruit me into this?"

"You can see how serious these guys are," she said, gesturing to the Hart boys and the other men standing around the room, all with guns on their hips. "Please tell me you're going to cooperate."

I leaned forward. "What. Do. You. Want. From. Me."

"I have one more mission for you," she said as she picked up her Newports and shook one out of the pack.

"Why me?" I stood up. "Why me!"

Warren stepped in to light her cigarette.

"Because I can trust you," she said, blowing smoke over my head.

I waved the smoke away. "What makes you think that? After all this."

"Because you're a good girl. You always have been. If you help me get through this, we can all go on with our lives."

"That's what you said last time. If I could get that information for you, they would let you go."

"I know, honey, but like I said, that was just a test. I promise, just do this for me and I won't ask you for anything else."

She put on a good show and I would have preferred to believe her. But I couldn't. "I'm sorry, Mom. I can't help you."

She threw down her cigarette and crushed it angrily. "Don't push me, Cal, or you'll be sorry."

"Mom!"

"You better listen to me carefully."

I stood up and backed away from her.

"I have eyes on your girlfriend."

I turned my back on her and took deep breaths to calm down. "I don't know what you're talking about."

"Jane," she said. "I know where she is. And I know what's going on between you two."

More deep breaths. I realized everyone in the room was staring at me.

"I also know it wasn't your fault. That Jane is a predator who needs to be disciplined."

"What do you mean by that?"

"You know what I mean," she said, getting close to me and whispering harshly into my ear. "You're going to do exactly as I say."

I doubled over, put my hands over my ears, thought about screaming as loud as I could, but I knew it wouldn't matter. "Leave me alone."

But she just stood there, towering over me. "Do you know what they do to cure homosexuals?"

I went after her, trying for her throat, but one of her henchmen pulled me back. I knew what she was talking about. It came up in Sunday school. They told us about shock therapy and even lobotomies to "shock the gay away."

"I can't believe you!"

"You listen to me, Cal," she said, in my face again. "You cooperate or I will make sure that girl gets shipped off to a camp for deviants like her who try to corrupt innocent children like you."

"You're insane! Jane's parents would never let that happen!"

"They hauled her off to boarding school, didn't they?"

I was seething. I wanted to smack the smug look off her face.

"I need to call Ted, Jane's brother. If I don't, Jane's going to think something happened to me and call the police."

"Nice try, sweetheart, but I'm not falling for that."

There was a volcano inside me and it was about to explode.

"I do have an idea, though, for how Jane can improve her standing in my eyes," Mom said.

"You are so full of it," I said.

"Don't talk to your mother that way," she said, pulling up two chairs and pushing me into one as she sat in the other. "Now, I'm going to explain what I need you and Jane to do."

I stared at the floor. I didn't want to see her face.

"Jane's father has access to the codes that unlock a secret petroleum reserve that's kept underground in Palo Duro Canyon. The plant manages that reserve for the federal government and he's the head honcho of the plant. We've been trying to get access to that reserve for months now."

"This is something different from the gas syphoning you've been doing?"

"Don't worry about the details," she said. "The less you know, the better."

"I don't know how Jane and I could possibly help you with this...reserve, or whatever it is."

"I need you to get the access codes," she said.

"How?"

"Talk to Jane. See what she can find out. Then get yourself into the plant."

I didn't respond.

"Find an excuse to go to work with your dad. He's on evenings this week."

"Do you really think this top-secret code is going to be sitting out on a desk somewhere?"

"Here's what I think," she said. "You're a pretty good detective, and there's a lot on the line, so I think you'll figure it out."

"Tell me the truth. Nobody's making you do this."

"Get her back to town," she said to Warren.

As I sat alone, waiting for my ride, I caught a glimpse of Hank Hart. He came through a door in the back of the warehouse, spotted me and came over. I hadn't really gotten that good a look at him before. He was much handsomer than I had thought. His eyes were intense, full of energy.

"There's something I want you to know," he said. I didn't say anything—just waited. "I came after your mother. She never would have gotten into this if I hadn't come along. She's a good woman."

He seemed to want a response. "You sure could have fooled me. She seems into it. In a big way."

"She didn't seek it out."

"Why don't you let her go?"

"She could walk out right now if she wanted to," he said. "Now, you get on back home. Do what she's asked you to do and everything will be fine."

"The Rangers said you put that envelope in our mailbox so I could figure this out."

"Actually, it was your girlfriend I was fishing for. Now you know why."

He walked away while one of the other men blindfolded me and took me back to a waiting truck. *Oh my god. All along it was Jane he wanted, through me!* He was clever, all right. The Texas Rangers hadn't thought of that angle. So far, he was winning.

Warren dropped me off a few blocks from school. When I got there, I checked in with the principal's office and told them I had been sick that morning. I was still shaky from the barrage of crap coming at me from all directions. The secretary told me I didn't look too good and maybe I shouldn't have come in at all. Walking down the hall, trying simply to put one foot in front of the other and keep my balance, I ran smack into the captain of the cheerleading squad.

"Hey, Cal. You know you have to show up for practice or you're going to be off the squad."

"Oh, yeah, sure," I said. "I know. I understand. Sorry about that. I'll be there tonight."

Funny how a few weeks ago I thought getting to cheerleading practice was my biggest problem in life.

"Homo," someone said as he passed by me in the hall.

I looked up to see a group of girls laughing and looking back at me. I felt like someone had sliced me with a knife. First, I was embarrassed and ashamed, and then I was angry. I wanted to go back and yell something awful at them, but instead, I turned down another hallway. School was beginning to feel like prison.

I had to walk to practice that night because Dad was working the evening shift and my bike had a flat I couldn't fix on the spot. Funny, but it was a relief to be there. I tried to forget everything else and just cheer.

"Nice handspring!" the captain said. "Have you been working on that?"

"Thanks!" I said. "Yeah, you know, I want to try out for the varsity next year."

Where did that come from? I hadn't worked on it at all and I had no intention of doing this again.

"You should!" she said.

Mrs. Anderson, the mother in charge of the squad, approached me as she was gathering up her things at the end of practice.

"How are things at home, Cal?" she asked.

"Uh, well—"

"You're at your dad's, right?"

"Yeah. It's fine."

"Let me know if you need any help."

"Sure," I said. "Thank you."

"Do you need a ride home?"

"That would be great. Dad's working late so I was hoping someone could give me a lift."

"Jennifer!" she called to her daughter. "Come on, let's go. We're giving Cal a ride."

I sat in the backseat, responding politely to questions from Mrs. Anderson while Jennifer faced forward, ignoring me.

"What do you hear from your mother, dear?"

I didn't have a story prepared so I had to think fast. "She's... doing some training. Getting another certification for her accounting stuff."

"Oh, I see. When will she be back?"

Jennifer looked back, rolling her eyes as if to say, "Please excuse my mother's annoying questions."

"You know, I'm not sure. But it's fine. I'm okay at my dad's."

When we got to Dad's apartment, I thanked her for the ride.

"Cal," she said as I was one foot out of the car. "God loves the sinner but hates the sin."

I was confused and tried to get Jennifer's attention, but she wouldn't make eye contact.

"Homosexuality is a sin."

"I don't know what you're talking about," I said and practically jumped out of the car.

"God will forgive you, but you have to repent," she said, leaning across Jennifer to shout at me through the passenger window.

I turned away from the car and started walking.

"We love you, Cal. It's our Christian duty!"

I kept walking, not looking back. What the heck? Christian duty? *It's your Christian duty to leave me alone.* Inside I found a note from Dad telling me he had bought my favorite TV dinners. I took one out of the freezer and heated it up in the oven. I sat at the kitchen counter, numb and unable to eat anything, playing with the food in the foil tray. The telephone rang and I answered it, expecting it to be Dad checking in.

"Cal, it's me!" Jane's voice sounded hushed and frantic. "Thank god you're okay."

"Hey, I'm hanging in there, barely."

"Why weren't you there at the time we said?"

"Are you crying?"

"Of course, I'm crying! I've been crazy worried about you!"

"You won't believe what's happening."

"Didn't you give your mom what she was looking for?"

"That whole thing wasn't even real."

"What?"

"She was messing around with me. It turns out what they really want has something to do with what your dad does."

"How?"

"Something about that petroleum reserve thing. Do you know anything about it?"

"A little," Jane said. "But why?"

"The gang just figured out that it's there. It's way bigger than the gas syphoning thing they've been up to so far. I think we can use this to trip them up once and for all. If we play it right."

"I don't know," Jane said. "I don't like it."

"I don't like it either, but I feel like I don't have a choice."

"What do you mean?"

"I don't want to scare you, but my mother threatened me with the most awful things today. It has to do with you. The gay thing."

"Jesus Christ," Jane said. "Sick."

"I have to take her seriously. If I don't come up with something, she could make trouble for you."

"What is it they want?"

"Some kind of codes—security codes. If they have them, they can get access to the reserves. Or at least that's what they think."

"Good luck with that."

"I know, but is there anything you can think of that might help?"

"Well," Jane said, "I never thought this would come up, but I think I know what your mom is talking about."

"How do you know?"

"When we first moved to town, I overheard my dad on the phone. I didn't mean to. I was in his library looking for something and he didn't realize I was there. I heard him talk about access codes. When he saw me, he went white as a ghost. He swore me to secrecy. Told me I had to forget what I'd heard."

"This sounds super serious."

"It's national security, Cal. We can't mess around."

"I understand. My plan will protect national security by setting up the Brazos River Gang to be caught and put away."

"I don't know. It could backfire. I can't believe we're in the middle of this."

"I get it. It's risky. Really risky. I don't blame you if you don't want to tell me."

"Wait," Jane said. "Who says you have to give them the real thing? You're setting them up anyway so the Texas Rangers can catch them."

"Yeah, but it has to look real."

"Here's what I know. Half of the code is in a notebook in the monitoring room at the plant. The other half is in a safe place outside the plant. My dad would never tell me where that is—for my own safety."

"Is this something I could memorize when I find it?"

"No. It's too complicated. But do you have a Polaroid camera?"

"My dad does."

"Get yourself into that room and use your charms to get a picture of that code in the notebook. That should be good enough to lure them in."

"I'll be so glad when this is all over," I said.

"Hey, I have to go. They're calling lights out here."

"Don't worry," I said. "I promise everything will be okay."

"Cal," she hesitated. "I...it's just that...I love—"

The line went dead as I glanced at the clock and watched it turn to ten p.m. As I hung up the phone, I decided on a plan, for better or worse. I couldn't sleep, so I waited up for Dad. He got off at eleven p.m. on the evening shift.

"Can I go to work with you tomorrow night?" I asked him after he put away his things in the closet. "I have a science project and we're supposed to research something from the real world."

"Sure," he said, "but do you know what you're looking for?"

Do I ever.

"I figure you can show me what you do for work. You know, let me see some gauges and instruments and I can write something up."

"All right, I'll pick you up from school and we'll go," he said. "Now you should get to bed."

I went to sleep feeling guilty that I was going to use my dad this way. But I couldn't risk my mother going after Jane. Her words rang in my ears. *Shipped off to a camp for deviants like her.*

CHAPTER TWENTY-SIX

"Ready?"

It was Dad, pulling up to the front of the high school as I walked out.

"Let's do it."

I pretended to be enthusiastic about the fake science project. We pulled into the plant campus through an iron security gate. The place smelled of a sickening sweet chemical mixture. I was used to it from the way his work clothes smelled, and the stench could be detected from miles away, but this close, it nauseated me.

"How do you work in this smell?"

"You get used to it."

"Gross."

We parked in the parking lot and walked to his building. He showed me the locker room where the men changed into jumpsuits. He handed me the smallest size, which was still way too big for me.

"You gotta wear it while you're here."

I took it into the ladies' restroom, as there was no locker for women, since they worked in the clerical offices in another building. Dad had brought my boots with him. I took my notebook and a pen and did my best to look like I was on a research project.

"Okay," I said, stepping into the hallway where he waited. "Where's your work area?"

"This way," he said, our steps echoing down the cinderblock hallway.

He took me into a room full of instrument panels, each with dozens of dials and gauges and meters with needles measuring who knows what. They kept the temperature super cold because of the machinery. Despite the jumpsuit, I was still cold, my teeth chattering a little. There were two other men in the room, each with clipboards marking sheets that looked like graph paper. I took notes about the room, not just for my fake project, but also to get me thinking and lead me to some sort of bright idea as to how to locate the code I was supposed to find.

"What's this?" I pointed to what looked like a leather-bound atlas.

"That's the *National Petroleum Registry*," Dad said. "It's maps and geological data on just about everything you'd ever want to know about oil in the whole world."

"Wow. Can I look at it?"

"I don't know why not. It's pretty technical. I don't think it'll mean much to you."

I opened the book and paged through it, getting an idea of how it was organized. It was indexed by region, then by country, then by specific categories like total oil production, crude oil production, refinery capacity and proven reserves. I found a section all about Texas, and there I noticed a page called *Strategic Petroleum Reserve*.

"Clear as mud?" Dad said from across the room, looking at a gauge and writing something down.

"Yeah," I said. "But it's giving me some ideas for my report."

I saw a reference to Palo Duro Canyon and thought this could be it. It was jargony, but it seemed to say that the government had made a decision to hide a certain amount of petroleum in Palo Duro Canyon as a hedge against OPEC countries' manipulation of the oil market. The reserve was secured by a complicated code, not guarded by people, so as not to call attention to the exact location. But I couldn't see a code or a reference as to how to find the code.

I closed the book and looked around the room. Back in a corner I hadn't noticed before was a bank of monitors, small black-and-white television sets. One of the men was sitting at a desk watching them. This might be what Jane was talking about.

"Mind if I watch?" I asked him.

"Go ahead," he said, pointing to a chair next to him. "My name's Bud."

As I sat down, Bud straightened up in his chair. "Your dad's the best boss out here."

He was young, probably only in his early twenties. He smoothed his shirt and ran his fingers through his short-cropped hair. I caught him looking at me for a second too long and thought he might try flirting with me.

"Really?"

"He's saved my butt more than a few times."

"Huh," I said. "What do you know?"

"Yeah, I probably would have been fired by now if he didn't have my back."

My dad really is a good guy.

"What is all this stuff you've got going here," I asked, pointing to the bank of little television-looking machines.

"These monitors, most of them, are security cameras around the plant," he said. "But this one, it's top secret."

"What's it for?"

"Hmm...I really shouldn't say."

"C'mon. I'm just curious. I won't put it in my report."

He thought it over. "It's Palo Duro Canyon," he said quietly. "There's a vault out there. Full of oil."

"Wow," I said. "What's it for?"

"In case the bad guys cut us off," he said, his eyes narrowing.

"Has anyone ever tried to break in?"

He shook his head vigorously. "No way. It's on lockdown like you wouldn't believe."

"I don't know," I said. "I bet if somebody was really smart, they could figure it out."

"It's foolproof," he said. "They had this math guy from Massachusetts or somewhere come up with this mile-long equation or, I don't know, something like that."

I started laughing.

"I'm serious, girl," he said, taking a key to open a drawer and reaching in for a notebook. "Look at this."

He showed me a long, complicated string of what looked like calculus computations.

"I see what you mean," I said.

"Damn right."

"Hey," I said. "All this research is making me thirsty. Do y'all have Cokes around here somewhere?"

"Back in the locker room. I'll get you one. Could use one myself."

He got up and I held my breath as I watched to see if he would leave the drawer unlocked. He did, and as soon as he was out of sight, I grabbed the notebook. I took the Polaroid out of my bag and snapped a picture, then another and another just to be sure. I just got the camera back in my bag when Dad came around the corner.

"Gettin' some good stuff?" he asked.

I closed my notebook. "Perfect," I said. "I can write my report now."

I fell asleep in the breakroom waiting for Dad's shift to end. But when we got home, my mind was running wild as I hit the pillow. I knew what I had to do and I couldn't let myself think about the consequences to my mother.

"I don't have anything yet," I said the next morning to one of the Hart boys who was lurking in the shadows near the entrance to the high school.

My strategy for now was delay. I didn't feel right about any of this, but so far I hadn't come up with another way out. I knew

I only had another day or two before they really upped the pressure on me.

"Rachel's back home!" someone said as I made my way through the crowded halls.

That was good news, but I immediately wondered why she hadn't called me if she was back from Dallas. The school day dragged on for what felt like an eternity. When I got home, I ran to the telephone and dialed her number. Her father answered.

"I'm sorry, Cal, but Rachel is resting now. It would be better if you didn't call her."

"Dad!"

I heard Rachel in the background.

"Let me talk to her!" Rachel said.

"Goodbye, Cal."

Her father hung up the phone. So the adults were trying to keep us all away from each other for their different reasons. I knew a way around that. Rachel and I had long ago figured out how to come and go through our bedroom windows. I hopped on my bike and headed over there. She opened the window when I tapped on it.

"You look good," I said. She was her normal color again, and one sure sign she was herself—she had origami butterflies all over the room.

"Oh, my gosh, Cal. That's insane," she said when I told her everything my mother had asked me to do. "You shouldn't be dealing with this alone. You've got to go to the authorities."

"I can't."

"Why not? If you just tell them what's going on, they can protect you."

"It's not that. There's something else."

I stood up, looked in the mirror, and turned back to face Rachel.

"My mother threatened...threatened me about Jane. You know, about how Jane is."

She looked confused at first and then it dawned on her. "Oh, that's so mean."

"Yeah," I said as I plopped onto the edge of the bed.

"But what could she do to Jane?"

"I don't know if she could really do anything, but she scared me. I guess there are places where they try to turn people from being, you know, that way... She says she could get Jane sent to one. I can't take any chances with that."

"What if you got in touch with Bev?"

"That's exactly what I have in mind. She and I could work together on this and make up for what happened in Tyler."

"You should call her right now," Rachel said. "I've still got her home number. I bet she would accept a collect call."

Rachel picked up the phone and listened to make sure no one else was on it and then dialed the operator for a collect call. When Bev accepted the charges, we huddled on the receiver.

"You should have called me right away," Bev said, scolding. "This is a whole different level from syphoning gas."

"I know," I said. "I'm sorry, it's just that I am so scared about Jane."

"Fine," she said, "but no more secrets. This is the national petroleum reserve. I can't for the life of me figure out how they know about it at all, much less where it is. I don't know how they think they can pull off an attack there. It's a suicide mission."

"They seem so sure of themselves. My mom was almost cocky. I wonder if we're missing something."

"Maybe they're working with another group, a much more sophisticated group. But whatever it is, it's a very big mistake."

"It's Cal I'm worried about," Rachel said. "Her mother has put her in a terrible position. She's been handling it all alone. Can you protect her?"

"This kind of thing is way beyond the scope of the Rangers. I'm sure the next thing will be to call in the FBI. I'll talk to my superiors about providing protection for Cal."

"Something's got to happen fast," I said. "They're expecting me to get them the code. I can't stall much longer."

"I'll do my best, but in the meantime, tell me everything you remember. You said they took you to a warehouse somewhere," Bev said. "What can you tell me about that?"

"All I know is it was about forty-five minutes from town. I checked my watch when they took the blindfold off. I don't know which direction, but it was a big building with really high ceilings."

"Like an airplane hangar?" Bev asked.

"Maybe. I've never seen one."

"Those are some good clues," Bev said.

"What about Jane?" I asked.

"She's safe where she is. I think your mother is bluffing. She'd give herself away if she tried to pursue that."

"If you're sure—"

"Just keep your wits about you. I'll get things moving immediately."

"This is so much worse than I thought," I said after we hung up the phone. "I can't understand why my mother is doing this to me. And Jane. And even you."

"I hate to say this, but it seems like she just doesn't care what happens to us."

"Right. And I'm starting not to care what happens to her."

CHAPTER TWENTY-SEVEN

I was almost back home from Rachel's when a truck came to a sudden stop at the corner and two men jumped out and dragged me inside. I closed my eyes, not bothering to resist.

"Cal," my mother said, sitting in the front seat.

I jerked to attention, looking at her.

"You have the code. Give it to me."

I didn't move at first.

"Now!"

I dug around in my book bag for the Polaroid pictures. I handed them to her.

"You can let me go now," I said.

"Oh, no, honey. You're coming along for the ride, as insurance in case this information is bogus."

"But—"

Oh, boy. I had to think. Had to figure out a way to escape. They hadn't blindfolded me this time. Looking out the window, I realized we were headed out of town in the direction of the canyon. I had an idea. There was a big culvert near there where we'd played as kids. It led to a sewer drain we used as a secret passage from that part of town back to our neighborhood.

I looked over at the door handle and in a split second decided to make a run for it. I went hard at the door, pushed it open and dove out. I got up and ran as fast as I could, heading toward a brush-covered entrance to the culvert. One of Mom's goons came after me. I was lucky. He slipped in the sandy dirt and I sprinted ahead, sliding into the culvert and pulling the brush over the entrance behind me. I stayed still for a while to make sure I'd lost him. I laid flat, perfectly silent. As I resisted the instinct to gag on the dank smell of the storm sewer, I heard him huffing and puffing and swearing. After a while, it was quiet.

I ran through the culvert, tripping over something and falling hard, skinning my hands and elbows. I got back to the neighborhood and Rachel's window, my heart beating out of my chest.

"What the heck?" she said when she saw me.

I was covered in dirt and leaves and must have looked like some kind of combat soldier. I described what happened through broken breath.

"Thank goodness you got away!"

"For now," I said.

"You probably shouldn't stay here. Isn't this one of the places they would look?"

"You're right. I can't go home either. I wish Bev had been more help. I need a solution right now."

"I wonder if Jane could help," Rachel said.

I called Grandma and asked her to check on her "niece" again. Within half an hour, Jane called Rachel's number.

"I've already been thinking about this," Jane said. "I knew you wouldn't be safe there. I want you to come up here."

I was confused. "How would we pull that off?"

"I have a credit card. I've checked it and it's still good. My parents haven't closed it. They probably forgot about it."

"Hmm. You mean take a bus up there? Or a train?"

"I mean take an airplane," Jane said.

"Fly?"

"You could fly to Syracuse and I could meet you."

"I don't know. Then what?"

"I haven't really figured everything out. I just know it's not safe for you to stay there. Give me an hour or so and I'll call you back."

While we waited, I cleaned myself up as best I could in Rachel's room. She brought me a washcloth from the bathroom since her dad was in the house somewhere. We were about the same size, so I borrowed some clothes and a small suitcase. She gave me a baseball cap and some sunglasses and I wore a jacket turned up around my neck.

"That's good," Rachel said, nodding approvingly at my disguise.

"I've booked you on a flight tomorrow morning," Jane said when she called back. "It's too late to get you here tonight, but you have to get to Amarillo so you can take the first flight in the morning. You can take the bus. Just be careful no one sees you. I got you a room at the airport motel. The bus makes a stop there. I used a fake name and paid for it already. The reservation is in the name Samantha Perkins."

I took a deep breath as I prepared to leave. Then I gave Rachel a hug and jumped down from her window. She dropped the suitcase out, waving me off, wishing me luck. I thought about Mom. I didn't feel bad. She got what she wanted out of me. Whatever happened next was all on her.

I walked through alleys and side streets on my way to the bus station. I had been there once when Mom and I went to Amarillo with some other moms and daughters to see *2001, A Space Odyssey*. I can't remember why we all took the bus. I guess it was supposed to be fun, but I remember being a little scared on the way home late at night.

Rachel had lent me enough money for the bus and a little extra for snacks and unexpected expenses. Jane said I would have to change planes twice, first in Dallas and then in Chicago. I couldn't believe I was going to get on a plane by myself! Not just one, but three. The more I thought about it, the more jittery I became and my palms began to sweat so much I almost couldn't hold onto the suitcase.

I got on the bus, breathing deeply to relax. I wanted a seat by myself, but it was crowded. I ended up next to a fat lady who smelled really bad. She was sweaty and farted a lot too. She was nice, though, and she shared her candy bars with me.

I got off at the motel and checked in without a problem. I stood in the shower for a long time, just enjoying the water washing over me. I still had the culvert dust in my fingernails. It felt good to get clean, and I slept better that night than I had in weeks.

I took the shuttle to the airport terminal right after breakfast and went to the ticket counter to pick up my ticket. They asked if I was okay to fly by myself. I lied and said I did it all the time to visit my aunt in New York. By now, with people all around me excited to be on their way to some distant city, I felt more at ease. I picked up a magazine in the waiting area so I would have something to read.

We got on the plane and I had a seat on the aisle in the back. The flight to Dallas Love Field was a little bumpy, but I thought it was fun. It felt like a roller coaster. The stewardess, a very pretty blonde, kept asking me if I was okay. The bumps didn't bother me at all. We got there in a little more than an hour. My layover at Love Field was enough time to eat lunch. I spotted McDonald's and couldn't believe my luck! We didn't have one at home. We had to go to Amarillo for that. I didn't want to spend the money for a Big Mac, so I got a regular hamburger and french fries. Those fries, drenched in ketchup, were the best thing I'd ever put in my mouth.

They called the flight to Chicago and this time my seat was closer to the front and on the window. I sat next to a couple who were going to visit their grandchildren in Chicago. They asked me a lot of questions about myself, so I made up a whole fake life. I told them my name was Samantha and that I was an archer and I was planning to try out for the Olympics in 1976. They were fascinated by that. I said I was going to upstate New York to get fitted for a special bow and arrow that I would use for the tryouts. I was having such a good time being someone else, I almost felt guilty about it.

But on the flight from Chicago to Syracuse, all I could think about was Jane and this whole ridiculous situation. Was this really a good idea, going to New York? What the heck did I think I was doing, anyway? I'm just a no-name kid from Texas. I'm not an Olympic athlete. I began to think this was all a big mistake. I was so deep in thought when the stewardess came by that she had to ask me three times what I wanted to drink.

Jane had told me she was meeting me at the gate. I had no idea how she could leave school. What if she wasn't there? I got a tight feeling in my chest, almost a panic attack. I worried I would hyperventilate again, but, when I walked off the plane, there she was. She hugged me so hard it hurt.

"I can't believe you're here. Was the flight okay? Were you scared?"

"Everything was fine," I said. "I wasn't scared once we got going. The stewardesses are all nice." She picked up my suitcase and headed for the exit. I felt dizzy. "Where are we going? How did you get away from school?"

She took my hand. "Everything's fine. You're here with me now," she said, steadying me with her gaze.

"Are you sure?"

"Yes. Don't worry about my school. It's not like a prison. I finished my classes, so I just took a cab here. As long as I'm there for dinner, no one will even notice."

"And what about me? You can't just parade me around."

"I know. I can hide you in my room for one night. My roommate is okay with it. But tomorrow we're going to have to do something different. And I have a lead on something, so don't worry."

The unfamiliar surroundings weighed on me and I felt my confidence draining away. The accents were so different from mine, and the people seemed hurried. They were loud and a little rude, so I stayed close to Jane as we made our way through the crowd to the taxi line.

"Now what's wrong?" she said.

"Nothing, I...it's just I'm...I don't know, having second thoughts, I guess."

She put her hands on my shoulders and made me look her in the eye. "This was right. Remember the last thing that happened to you in Texas? You were kidnapped. It's a miracle you got away."

"You're right," I said. "I just don't know where we're going with this."

"I want you to be safe. And I think you're safer here with me than you are there."

"I understand, but my dad is probably going crazy wondering what happened to me. It's not like me to disappear like that."

"We can get a message to him. Rachel can let him know you're okay."

"I guess so, but he's not going to give up trying to find out where I am."

"Maybe you should tell him what you know about your mom, so he can understand how dangerous it would be for you to be there."

"No. I don't want him to know this latest crazy plan she's got with Hank. He might try to stop her, which would just end badly for him."

She put her arm around me. "You're putting a good face on this, but I know it's getting to you. It has to be."

I fought back tears. I didn't want to cry. Not over my mother. Not ever again. "As much as I hate her right now, I would still save her if I could. They're walking into the trap I helped to set. I wish I could warn her. Tell her to get out before it's too late."

"Okay. Well, maybe that's what we should do then."

I caught my breath. "What? How?"

"I'm not sure. We need to think. Brainstorm some ideas. Let's get back to my room and work through this. There has to be a way."

We got in a cab. I had never been out of the Southwest before, and I was surprised by how green it was. And the mountains, as they called them, were so small. The more I took it all in, the better I felt. The air was different here, wetter. I was sweating a little, even though the driver had the windows down and the breeze blew my hair back. We held hands. Soon we were approaching the school on the long drive up to the entry.

"Pull around there to the back of the building," Jane said to the driver.

He followed her directions and we got out of the cab without anyone seeing us. We were behind Jane's dorm building, and we arrived at her room without passing too many other students and no adults.

Her room was very small—even smaller than my office room at my dad's. The beds looked like bunks, but the bottom was a couch, not a bed. Her roommate had decorated her side all in pink—pink sheets, pink pillows, pink stuffed animals, a pink clock, even the posters she had hanging on her wall had pink borders.

"We call her Pinkie," Jane said.

I laughed. Jane's side of the room was mostly lavender and yellow and she didn't have anything on the walls.

"I don't want to get too comfortable," she said. "With any luck I won't be here next semester." We sat cross-legged on her couch, facing each other.

"Here's what I started thinking about," she said. "Isn't Rachel's mom friends with your mom?"

"Frankie? Yes, they've been friends as long as me and Rachel."

"Do you think Joyce might still be in touch with her?"

"Hmmm. I don't know."

"She must still have some connection to her old life. I think it's worth a shot. We should ask Rachel to pay close attention to her mom's conversations. If they're still in touch, Rachel might overhear Frankie talking to Joyce and get a clue as to how we can get in touch with her."

"Okay. Can we call from here?"

"No. We can't have a private conversation here. And I'm only allowed a few minutes of long distance a day. But I have an idea."

"Let's hear it."

"We can't stay here more than one night," she said. "It's too hard to hide you. So..." She reached over and pulled a road atlas down from her bookshelf. She opened it up to New York. "Here's where we are and here's where I know of a place we can stay. We can use it as our base of operations." She pointed to Lake Placid in the Adirondack Mountains.

"Base of operations?"

"Yes. We have a mission to finish."

I shook my head and hugged her. "You are amazing. But what is this place? And how do you explain being away from school?"

"The school part is easy enough because the teachers have training for a few days and we don't have class. As for the Adirondacks, one of the girls here has a family camp there. They call it camp. It's a house. She said we could stay there. There's no one there now, but they haven't closed it for the season yet. They have a key hidden under a rock somewhere."

"How do we get there?"

"That's the tricky part," Jane said. "We have to hitchhike." I must have looked like I saw a ghost because Jane grabbed my hands and smiled really big. "Relax, we can do this."

I had a sensation of weightlessness, like stepping into the air and being suspended for a second before you know you're going to fall and shatter into a thousand pieces. "Are you sure?"

"I know this is scary," Jane said. "But we have to stay on the move. My parents are going to figure out I used that credit card. Your dad is going to be hounding the authorities to find you. If we're going to warn Joyce, we have to do this."

"I guess you're right. We've come this far. We have to keep going."

Jane brought me dinner from the cafeteria that night. It was mystery meat with mashed potatoes and broccoli. I didn't have much of an appetite, but I forced myself to eat. I figured I would need the energy. I slept on the couch with a sheet and pillow.

We got up before sunrise and before any of the grounds crew arrived at the school. We cut through the woods to the highway. The grass was wet with dew and the air was so cold we could see our breath. We had packed a few clothes into a backpack and had another one filled with snacks and some water. We carried a poster board that said Lake Placid. By the time we got to the road, the sun was coming up and there wasn't much traffic.

"How do we know we won't get picked up by an ax murderer?" I asked.

"We don't," Jane said. "But I've looked into it. Lots of people hitchhike around here and there's almost never any problem."

"Almost."

"Compared to what you've been up to lately, this is a piece of cake."

We didn't have any options anyway. It was too far to take a cab and there weren't any buses that would get us there. We held up the sign and stuck out our thumbs every time someone came by. We walked for almost an hour before someone slowed down. It was a girl, not much older than us, driving a pickup truck. She told us to get in.

Her name was Jewell and she worked in Oneida. She said she could take us that far and could drop us at a good spot to get another ride.

"You guys aren't from around here, huh?" she said, but she didn't wait for an answer. "I been here all my life. Ain't never been nowhere. Steve, he talks about moving to New York City, but he's full a shit. He don't know anything about the City. He works in the factory, just like everybody else around here. He pissed me off last night. Come home drunk, all mean and nasty, just about dropped the baby when he picked her up. She's only a year old. She's started to walk. She's a doll. Looks just like him. She stays with my mom while I'm at work. We live with her. Steve says he's gonna get us an apartment, but he's full a shit about that too. He don't save a dime. What he don't drink away, he gambles away. I'm gonna throw him out. I just have to get the last hundred bucks he owes me. I make him pay me back ten bucks a week. If I can stand it that long."

Jane and I never said a word the whole ride. She dropped us on the highway near a truck stop and said we should be careful who we got in with. "There's some lady truck drivers come through here. You girls should get with one a them if you can," she said. "Watch yourselves."

We used the restroom in the truck stop and looked around to see if we could find any female drivers. We didn't see any.

"Let's walk around the parking lot," I said. "Maybe we'll see somebody out there."

"What are you girls up to?"

It was a security guard. He was tall and skinny with leathery and sunburned skin that made it seem like he lived outside.

"Oh, nothing really," Jane said. "Just stretching our legs."

"Move along. You got no business among these trucks."

We headed back out toward the highway. When we got to the edge of the lot, we saw a woman climbing up into a rig. I waved to her.

"You girls looking for a ride?"

"We're headed to Lake Placid," I said. "Are you going that way?"

"So happens," she said. "Get in."

It was a fancy rig. It even had a sleeping area with two bunks behind the seats. It smelled new. We were so high up in that cab! I sat in the middle between her and Jane. There were so many gauges and meters on the dashboard that it looked like a science lab. And there were outlets to plug in whatever you wanted to bring along. You could live in it if you wanted.

"Man, that is cool," I said.

"Sounds like you might want to learn how to operate one of these rigs," Darlene said.

"I never thought about it before. How do you learn it?"

"There's trucker's school. It's tough. You have to be strong. And you have to be on your toes. There's all kinds of dangers out here on the road."

Jane had fallen asleep on my shoulder.

"What's the scariest thing that's ever happened?"

She didn't even take a second to think about that one. "I had a runaway once. I was driving east into Denver over Loveland Pass. It was March. A snowstorm came up out of nowhere, like it does out there. The wind hit me from the back and the trailer started to fishtail. I was new, and I hadn't been through something like that before. The rig got ahead of me and I had to pull off onto a runaway ramp. Scared the beejeezus out of me."

I got the shivers. "Wow. I've seen those ramps. I always wondered if trucks really run up on them."

"Oh, yeah, they do. And sometimes they miss."

Darlene was pulling a grocery delivery for Lake Placid, so she got us all the way into town. We jumped out at the store where she stopped, but we still had to get to the house, which was out on the lake.

"Maybe somebody doing their grocery shopping is headed out to the lake," I said.

We picked up some supplies—milk, cereal, peanut butter and jelly, bread, and some hot dogs. Jane took the poster and put the address of the house on it. We held it up at the driveway of the store parking lot. It didn't take long for someone to roll down their window and ask if we needed a ride.

She was in her fifties, probably, with wispy blond-gray hair and a big easy smile. "Hop in, girls," she said.

She had a car full of groceries.

"I'm Marge. You can help me unload. I live just down the block from the Jacksons. How do you know them?"

"I'm at school with Jenny Jackson," Jane said. "She's letting us stay there for a few days."

I waited for her to ask why, but she didn't. She just nodded and drove us out to the lake. We unloaded her car and helped her put away everything.

"You girls should come over for dinner one night this week. My boys will be here," she said, winking.

"That would be great," Jane said. "Let us know."

We walked down the block to the Jacksons' house. Jane knew a little of the history of it from what Jenny had told her.

"It was built in the twenties," she said. "They used these places for people who had tuberculosis. I guess the air was good for that. You have these big porches on the back where you can sit and breath it in."

The house was all wood—the floors, the paneling on the walls, and the ceilings with rafters extending high into the roofline. There were animal heads all over the walls and animal skins all over the floors. The place smelled musty mixed with cold fireplace ashes. There were six bedrooms, most of which had bunks or twin beds in them. There was a huge fireplace, the opening as tall as we were, in what Jane called the great room.

The bathrooms were small and had tiny sinks and bathtubs that sat on the tile floor. There was a dock leading to the lake. And that lake was amazing.

"Look at this!" I said.

The lake was lined with trees, like a forest shooting out of the water up a cliff all around it. I had never seen anything like it before, not even in Colorado.

"We can kayak on the lake tomorrow," Jane said.

"It's like I'm a million miles from home," I said.

"Speaking of home," Jane said. "Let's get Rachel on the phone. See what she can find out."

When we told Rachel our plan, she was all in. She would make a point of listening in on her mom's phone conversations to see if Joyce was in touch with her. I relaxed a little after that. At least we had a plan. I didn't feel totally helpless.

"But before you go," Rachel said as we were saying goodbye. "I don't want to scare you even more, but there's a reward out for information on Cal."

"What?" we both said.

"Yeah, it's on the radio, and I heard it's even in the papers back East. Because of Jane."

"That just means we have even less time than we thought," I said. "Get to work!"

We hung up the phone and, exhausted, looked through the rooms of the house to find one we liked. We picked one with twin beds and made them up with the rough cotton sheets and wool blankets that were in the closet. The mattresses were thick and heavy and not comfortable at all. But we didn't care. I could barely say goodnight as I pulled the covers up to my chin in the chilly air.

"Hey," Jane said, reaching her hand across the space between our beds. "You're a brave girl."

"Hmm?" I couldn't wake up enough to open my eyes. "I don't know why you say that."

"I love you," she said.

I was too far gone to respond.

CHAPTER TWENTY-EIGHT

We got up early the next morning and went kayaking. Jane told me it was called a tandem. I had never been in a kayak before. The lake was still and a fog lay across the surface, but eventually the sun rose higher and dissolved the fog. We paddled past house after house with docks onto the lake. I could not have felt further from my life. At the same time, I knew it was there and I knew I would have to face it again.

"Look!" Jane said.

Fish jumped through the surface of the water, flopping on their bellies.

"I bet we could catch one with our hands," I said.

"Don't—" Jane said, but I didn't listen.

I reached for the next one I saw, losing my paddle and my balance. I flipped the kayak over, throwing us both into freezing cold water.

"Oh my god! I can't believe you did that!"

We were close enough to our dock that we swam the kayak back to the shore and pulled it out, shaking like crazy from near hypothermia.

"I'm going to kill you!" Jane said.

She came after me and I ran onto the porch, pulling towels out of the bin and throwing one around her.

"I'm so sorry," I said.

"I'm getting in the shower. I think I'm going into shock."

She was shivering badly. We ran to the nearest bathroom and I turned on the faucet and pulled the shower tab up. I helped her get her clothes off and step into the claw-foot tub.

"Get in with me," she said. "You're just as cold."

I undressed and got in, still shivering. The hot water felt like heaven and we stood there for a long time soaking it in. Once we were warm again, she pulled me closer and kissed me. I melted and fused into her. I didn't want to turn the water off, not only because it felt so good, but because the air was chilly and we hadn't thought to get our bath towels out of the closet.

"I'll go," I said.

I ran to the hallway and brought back the bath towels. I hadn't let myself really look at her while we were standing under the water, but now I did.

"Give me that towel!"

"Sorry, I was just—"

"I hope you learned a lesson," she said when we were back in the bedroom.

She opened a drawer and found a couple of thick cable sweaters. "I'm sure Jenny won't mind."

"Can you make a fire?" I said, grinning as sweetly as I could. "You're so good at it."

She sneered at me. "You're lucky I like you so much."

She built the fire out of wood that was stored around the side of the house. It was roaring in no time. We lay on a bearskin rug in front of it. Soon the phone rang with Rachel's signal of two and a half rings. We called her back.

"Bingo," Rachel said.

"You heard them talking?" I asked, huddled on the receiver with Jane.

"Yes. My mom is losing her mind over this. She can't believe Joyce won't leave the gang."

"Did you figure anything out about where she is or how we can get in touch with her?"

"No, but I have an idea."

"Go ahead," I said.

"Why don't we ask my mom to help? She's so upset. If she knew Joyce is in even bigger trouble, wouldn't she want to help us get to her?"

"Maybe," I said hesitantly.

"We haven't told Rachel exactly where we are," Jane said. "Even if Frankie tells on us, they still don't know where we are. All she has to do is give us a phone number and a time to call Joyce."

"It's worth a try," Rachel said. "Unless y'all have another idea."

"Okay," I said. "See what you can do. If it backfires, just know that I owe you."

"I'll give you the signal when I'm ready to talk again."

Marge had invited us for dinner that night. Her two sons were right about our age and she wanted us to all meet. I wasn't that excited about going over there, but at least it would be a home-cooked meal, better than PB&J or hot dogs for dinner.

"Come in, girls," she said. "Meet my boys, Harry and Thomas."

It was awkward since Marge was pretty clearly trying to set us up as a double-date. Jane offered to help in the kitchen and I asked to look around outside. Harry and Thomas came out with me.

"Where's that accent from?" Thomas asked.

I felt a little embarrassed. I didn't think I was that obvious.

"Texas," I said.

"That's where you live?"

"Yeah. I'm visiting Jane. We know each other from home."

I walked out to the edge of the dock and stared up at the sky. It was a clear night and I could see a thousand stars. I thought about Mom. I wondered where she was—what she was thinking, whether she worried about me. Being away from there and having time to think was getting to me. Something welled up inside and I felt a cry about to force its way out. I couldn't let that happen, not in front of these strangers. I bolted back inside as fast as I could without running. I found Jane in the kitchen. By the look on her face, she could tell I was about to lose it.

"Hey," she said. "Here, shuck this corn."

It was good she gave me a job to do. I peeled the husks back and got rid of the silk. Then I smoothed the husks back on the cob. I ran water over them and asked for some foil. "I learned this from my grandmother," I told her. "You roast them in the husks. The water keeps them moist. It's really good this way."

The boys cooked steaks on the grill and roasted the corn. Marge made fresh asparagus, something I had never tasted before. She nudged me and asked if I thought her boys were cute. I nodded and asked what else we could do to help. She put us in charge of a lettuce and tomato salad. The more I worked in the kitchen, the more I relaxed. We set the table in the great room and took our seats.

Harry went for Jane and Thomas went for me. It was annoying. Jane and I played footsie under the table while we laughed at their silly jokes. When dinner was over, the boys asked us to go for a walk, so we did. The boys pushed at each other and generally acted stupid.

"We have a ski boat," Thomas said. "Do you want to go out tomorrow?"

"The water is freezing," I said.

"We have wet suits," he said.

I guess neither one of us could think of a reason not to, so we ended up agreeing to go out on their boat. We said goodbye to them and walked back to the house.

"That wasn't bad, huh?" Jane said.

"It was good. They're nice people."

"But you don't look so good."

"I'm nervous. I just wish this would all go away."

"It'll be over soon. One way or another."

We sat on the porch in the back, looking out on the lake, while Jane smoked a cigarette. "When this started, it was like a game. I really thought I could figure it out. That I could save her. Now I feel ashamed and silly for thinking I could be some kind of hero."

"Don't give up hope. Rachel may come through."

We stayed quiet for a long time. I sensed Jane wanted to come up with something to comfort me, but there was really nothing to say.

I reached for her hand. "I'm sorry for dragging you into the middle of all this."

"Don't be," she said. "First of all, you didn't drag me. I went after you, you know?"

"What do you mean?"

"Oh, c'mon. Do you think it was an accident that I was in the prayer garden that day?"

I smiled. "You were looking for me?"

"You bet I was. I had my eye on you for a while."

"I can't believe it!"

"I set my little trap and you fell right in." She smiled and squeezed my hand. "So don't be apologizing to me for anything."

Just then, Rachel signaled us to call her.

"Well?" I said, anxious.

"You have a date," she said. "Of course, Joyce doesn't know it's gonna be you calling. She'll think it's my mom."

"Was your mom mad about me running away? Did she say anything about that?"

"I wouldn't say she's mad. She just thinks the whole world has gone to hell. But she is hoping you can talk sense into Joyce."

"When are we supposed to call her?"

"Tomorrow at four o'clock. After that, you better be ready to move. I can't believe the Rangers or the FBI won't figure out where you are by then."

"That's probably right," I said, saying goodbye.

The next day, since we had to kill time until four p.m. anyway, we met up with Harry and Thomas at their dock.

"At least this will take your mind off things for a while. I think you'll like skiing."

I was nervous about the boat and the skiing. I didn't know how to ski. Of course, Jane was an expert. She assured me that it wasn't hard and that she would tell me exactly what to do.

She got in the water behind the boat and demonstrated. "Once you get your feet in the bindings, get the ski tips up out of the water. Hold the rope between the skis. Bend your knees. As the boat takes off, keep your knees bent until you're up on the water. Then straighten your legs."

She handed Harry one of the skis. "Slalom?" he asked.

She nodded. On only one ski, she popped up out of the water like a rocket.

"Look at her go!" Harry yelled.

I just shook my head. Was there anything Jane wasn't good at? I gave it a try, doing exactly what she said and it worked. I liked it well enough, and they all pushed me to do more. In the end I even tried to slalom and I managed to stay up for a few seconds.

"Awesome!" Jane called out.

They all congratulated me as they pulled me back into the boat. We ate the lunch that Marge had made for us as we sat out in the middle of the lake with our wetsuits peeled down to the waist. The boys had snuck some beers into the cooler so we all had one. Every time I tasted it, I got a little more used to it, and now I sort of like it.

"Do you like it out here?" Thomas asked, moving to sit next to me on the bench seat.

"Sure," I said. "Thanks for bringing us out here. It's really nice of you."

"You have really pretty skin," he said, touching my cheek.

I drew back and didn't say anything. He leaned toward me and tried to kiss me. I ducked away.

"Hey, that's a little fast," I said, sneaking a look at Jane, who frowned at me.

"Okay, we can take it slow," he said, moving even closer to me on the seat.

"I don't think she's interested at any speed," Jane said, giving him a disdainful look.

"That's kinda rude," Harry said to her.

"Sorry," I said, realizing I needed to head this off and smooth it over. "I…I have…I have a boyfriend."

"That's okay," Thomas said. "It's not like I'm trying to go steady. It's just a vacation thing."

When they finally took us back to the dock, I couldn't wait to get off the boat. They offered to have us for dinner again, but we thanked them and said we had other plans. As we stripped off the wetsuits, they were both trying to look at us without being obvious. I laughed as we slipped our clothes on as fast as we could.

"What's wrong with you?" Jane asked as we walked back into the house. "You practically invited him to make out with you."

"What are you talking about? I didn't do anything."

"With boys, you have to be crystal clear or they think you're saying yes."

"Don't be mad. I was just trying to be nice."

She pushed me up against the wall, pinning me, kissing me hard. "I can't stand the thought of anyone else touching you."

"You don't have anything to worry about, silly, so stop."

We dropped onto the couch and kissed until I realized it was time to make the call.

"I'm nervous," I said. "I feel like this is my last chance with her. How can I make her listen to me for once?"

"You can't make her do anything," Jane said. "All you can do is tell her what you know and hope for the best. It's not your fault if she won't listen."

"I know, but still, if I hadn't gone to the plant and taken those pictures, maybe they would have given up on this crazy idea that they can break into the petroleum reserve."

"Cal, listen to me. You are not to blame for anything here. I don't want to hear you talk like that ever again."

Jane lit a cigarette as I stood over the phone, poised to dial.

"Go ahead," she said. "You're already a minute late."

"Hello?" It was my mother's voice.

"It's me, Mom."

"Where the hell are you?"

"Mom, listen to me. I need to tell you something."

"What you need to do is get your butt back home. I don't know where you are or how you got there or even who you think you are. I'm not listening to this."

"Mom! Wait! The codes. They're not enough. You're headed into a trap!"

"What are you talking about?"

"What I got from the plant. It's only half of what you need."

"And how would you know that?"

Just then there was a brutal banging on the front door.

"What the hell?" Jane said, running to the door.

Before she could get to the door, it burst open and several cops pushed into the room. In the commotion, I realized Mom had hung up. I shouted uselessly into the phone.

"What's going on here," Jane asked. "You can't just barge in here."

"Carrie Ann Long. Jane Rawlings. You're under arrest."

"What? I don't understand," Jane said, backing up to hold my hand.

"You need to come with us. Get your things together."

Jane and I looked at each other helplessly. The policemen hurried us out and into a squad car. As they sped us away to the airport, I caught sight of Harry and Thomas, their arms crossed, watching us go.

"They did it," I said.

"What are you talking about?" Jane said.

"Harry and Thomas, and probably Marge. They turned us in."

Jane put her head on my shoulder and cried softly.

Jane and I were separated as soon as we landed in Amarillo. Apparently, the police in Texas weren't going to hold us. Jane's parents had sent separate cars for us. We managed a hug before they pushed us to our rides. Mine dropped me at my dad's.

"I don't know what to say to you, girl," he said as he came through the front door. "Have you lost your mind?"

"Dad, you've been right about Mom all along. I just kept thinking that if I could talk sense to her, she would get out of that mess and come back home."

"Well, I understand," he said. "I've felt that way about Joyce for a long time. I've tried to talk sense to her about all kinds of things. Truth is, I haven't been able to get through to her for years now."

"I'm sorry, Dad. I really am."

He hugged me and said, "You've done all you can do. Let it go."

CHAPTER TWENTY-NINE

"Cal!" Rachel said when I knocked on her door the next day. "Thank goodness you're back."

"I guess so," I said. "Things aren't exactly working out like I planned. But, hey, you look great. All back to normal."

"Tell me what you did up there. What was it like? What's happening with the gang? How did the police track you down?"

"One thing at a time," I said, sitting on her couch. "Bev got in touch with me this morning. She told me the Rangers are monitoring every move the gang makes, so I shouldn't worry about them coming after me."

"That sounds like good news."

"Yeah, they still expect them to hit the petroleum reserve any day now. I didn't get anywhere with Mom. So, if she's with them when they make that hit, I don't know how she'll survive."

"I'm so sorry."

"Jane says I've done all I can do. And Dad too."

"You have! And don't give up hope. There's a chance your words got through."

"I guess so."

"Where is Jane?"

They separated us in Amarillo and I assume she's at home."

"That sounds right. I overhead my parents talking, and it turns out that school in New York doesn't want her back. Once they found out she left the campus without her parents' permission, they decided she was too much trouble."

"Knowing Jane, that was part of her plan all along."

"I wouldn't put it past her. Her phone number's no good now," Rachel said.

"I know. I thought about Ted, but his number is unlisted. I think going over there is the only way. We have to sneak in somehow."

"Here we go, right back into hot water."

"Maybe you shouldn't go with me," I said. "You're just back to your old self. The last thing we need is a setback with you."

"Oh, I'm going with you. Are you kidding?"

We waited until sunset to make it less likely that anyone would notice us. Dressed all in black, we rode without our lights on.

"I feel like a cat burglar," Rachel said. "Like in that TV show. The one about a guy who used to be a thief and now he breaks into places as a good guy."

"Right. Well, I hope you're as good as he is."

We left our bikes in some bushes several yards away from the entrance to the property. We ran alongside the stone fence and reached the main house.

"I know what to do," I said. "If we can get into the kitchen, there's a dumbwaiter we can fit into, one at a time, and get up to her floor."

"Brilliant!"

"Let's hope so."

We crawled to the front side of the house, looking in the windows to see if her parents were there. We saw Jane's dad sitting in their family room, reading a book, but we didn't see her mom. It looked like maybe he was the only one home. We made our way around the house until we got to the kitchen. We didn't see anyone there. I tried the door. It was unlocked! I put my finger to my lips, signaling Rachel to be quiet. We tiptoed over to the dumbwaiter. Sure enough, it was just the right size for one of us. I pointed to the button that Rachel should push once I was inside.

"I'll send it back for you," I mimed.

I got inside and went up. The door opened automatically when I got to the top floor so I had to hope no one would be in the hallway to see me. It was dark and the hallway was empty. I sent the dumbwaiter back for Rachel, but after a few minutes it still hadn't come back. I wondered if she couldn't figure out how to send herself up. After a few more minutes, I gave up, hoping there wasn't a problem. Just as I walked away, she appeared.

"What happened?"

"Her dad came into the kitchen. I had to jump into the pantry and hide until he left."

"You're sure he didn't see or hear anything?"

"Sure as I can be. I waited until it was completely quiet. Nobody was in the kitchen when I got in this thing."

We crept down the hall to Jane's room. I knocked as quietly as I could and listened with my ear on the door.

"Jane," I said in a loud whisper. "Are you in there?"

There was no answer.

"Just open it," Rachel said.

Jane wasn't in her room, but I could tell she hadn't been gone long. The room smelled like her and I stood there, just breathing her in. There was a half-eaten sandwich on the table next to her bed. And the bathroom had recently been used for a shower.

"She's definitely been here," Rachel said. "I say we wait and see if she shows up."

"She's probably somewhere with her mom, right?"

We sat on the floor near the bed and talked in soft voices. After a while, we heard some activity in the hallway and I recognized Jane's voice. We rushed over to the closet, just in case she wasn't alone.

"I know that was tough," we heard her mother say, "but it's for your own good. Now goodnight."

When the door closed, we came out of the closet.

"Holy crap," Jane whispered. She grabbed both of us. "I can't believe you're here. How did you get in?"

We explained and she was very impressed with our cat burglary.

"Where were you? What was your mom talking about?" I asked.

She held her hands to her head and squeezed. "They're trying to shrink my brain."

"Not the shock."

"No, thank god. Just talk for now."

"What do they say?" Rachel asked.

"Just a bunch of BS about how God made the woman for the man, and you can't have a woman with a woman or a man with a man. Blah blah blah. That if I think I like girls, I have a mental illness and they will have to treat me."

"And what do you say?" I asked.

"I act like I know that and it's all fine. I say I don't like girls except as friends, like a normal person. So long as they let me out of there."

"Do they believe you?" I asked.

"I have to go back a few more times. He gave me this test and if I pass it three more times, I'll be cured forever, according to him."

"It's not fair that you have to lie, but it's probably the best thing to do," Rachel said. "Otherwise, they won't leave you alone. I had a cousin who was like that. He never could pass the test because he told the truth. They ended up doing something to him that made him lose his mind. He lives in a home now."

"Rachel's right. You don't have a choice. Just tell them what they want to hear."

"How far do I have to go with that? Find some guy, get married, have kids, fake my whole life?"

Rachel and I both stared at the floor.

"It's not like this everywhere," Jane said. "I've lived in LA. People I went to school with are from New York City. It's not normal or anything, but there are pockets here and there where people can be who they are. In San Francisco, they even have something called Gay Pride with parades and parties and they have fun."

"We can move there!" Rachel said. "When we're older I mean."

"You don't have to," I said. "You're not gay."

"I know, but I like gay people."

We heard a noise in the hallway.

"Quick, get in the closet," Jane said.

There was a knock on the door and then her mother opened it. "I just want to say how proud I am of you, honey. You're going to be fine. Everything will be back to normal soon."

"Sure, Mom. Everything is normal."

Jane gave us the all clear.

"Are you back in school here?" I asked.

"Starting next week," she said.

"Can we still see each other?"

"I don't see how. They're going to lobotomize me if they think I'm backsliding."

"There has to be a way," I said. "I'm not giving up. This isn't right."

"I never thought it would come to this. I wouldn't have been so obvious."

"It's your mom," I said.

"Yeah. My dad doesn't care. He's just keeping her off his back."

"Maybe we could change her mind."

"I don't think that's possible."

"Wait, what if you both had boyfriends," Rachel said.

I looked at Jane and thought about it.

"I think it could work! How could anyone complain? We have boyfriends and we all hang out together."

"I guess I could make that work, for a while, maybe," Jane

said. "But it's not a long-term solution. I can't live like this. I'm close to considering emancipation."

"What's that?" Rachel asked.

"It means you're on your own, out of your parents' control. An adult."

"Is that really necessary?" I asked, panicked at the thought of Jane off on her own somewhere.

"I don't think you quite get it, Cal. This is who I am. I don't want to hide or pretend. I've been doing that for too long. I guess it's not the same for you."

I put my arms around her and held her close. "I'm starting to understand. Give me time."

"Jane!" It was her mother calling from the hallway. "Come downstairs. I have something for you."

"You two get out of here," Jane said. "Be careful."

Jane unlocked her window and we went down the fire escape and made our way back to our bikes. I felt unsettled by our conversation. I had started to feel the reality of not being "normal," and I was not quite sure how to handle it.

CHAPTER THIRTY

My dad and I were getting along really well since I got back from New York. We talked about a lot of things, including how odd it was that neither Frankie or I had heard from Mom in about ten days. It was eerily calm for me after spending so much time looking over my shoulder in fear of being dragged off the street. I stayed in touch with Bev, but all she could tell me was that they were still monitoring the gang, waiting for them to make a move.

Meanwhile, Jane and I acted on the boyfriend idea. Jane started hanging out at football practice and flirting with the boys. Rachel and I stopped by a few times for moral support, but it made me feel sad to watch her. I could feel how humiliating it was for her. I wasn't even jealous because I knew it was me she wanted to be with.

It wasn't long until Jimmy, the star running back and captain of the football team, started hanging back after practice to talk to her. She told me about it during lunch in the cafeteria one day—one of the few places we got a chance to talk.

"He asked me out," she said. "So I guess the plan may work."

"Where are you going?"

"Just to the movies. Saturday night."

I stared into her eyes for a little too long.

"I miss you," I whispered.

"This is killing me," she said.

"I know. But it's the only way. I couldn't take it if they sent you away again."

"Meet me in the locker room after school. Girls track has practice, but it'll be all clear after they're dressed and on the field."

We met in the locker room and after all the girls had left for practice, we were alone together for the first time in weeks. She took my hand and pulled me into a shower stall in the back, pushing the thin cloth curtain across its track.

"I just want to look at you for a minute," she said. "I haven't dared to really look at you in school since we've been back. People would see right through me."

We stood there in the wet, musty, dank shower stall, in a world of our own where only the two of us existed. She wore a cotton miniskirt and a short-sleeved blouse with buttons in the front. I started to unbutton the shirt as I kissed her lips. She closed her eyes and I kissed her neck, her chest heaving deeply against me. When her lips found mine again, she cupped my head in her hands, kissing me gently through tears that slipped into my mouth as my whole body started to ache.

"Why are you crying?"

I looked at her, my own tears summoned up in sympathy. Before she could respond, we heard a door open and a locker squeak. Someone had bailed on practice. We stood still and quiet and waited for the silence again.

"I don't know how long I can do this," she whispered. "This town, these people, my own mother, are all so backward. We have to get away from here."

"You're scaring me," I said, starting to tremble. "We can't run away. They would find us and end up destroying us. We have to hold on. Get out of high school. Be free to go and do whatever we want. Please tell me you won't do anything crazy. Like that emancipation thing. Promise me."

She kissed me, nodding, but without much conviction. We left the locker room separately.

It wasn't long before Jane and Jimmy were a couple. I had to admire her acting ability. She was flawless, playing the part of the good girlfriend. She reminded me, often, that it was all for me. She even convinced her shrink and her parents that she was fully recovered from being gay. But she didn't like it at all that I had a boyfriend too.

I had accepted the attentions of that boy who had had a crush on me since seventh grade—Scott. He and I talked on the phone for hours every night.

"Why do you put so much effort into it?" Jane asked me one day when we met in the hall.

"I don't think I try any harder than you do," I said. "The more convincing we are at being straight, the less anyone cares how we act with each other."

"I just don't want you to convince yourself that you're straight."

"And I want you to trust me. This is working great. Don't we have another double-date this weekend?"

"Okay, okay. You're right."

I took a chance and gave her a quick kiss before running to my next class.

"Stop hogging the phone!"

Rachel yelled one night after one of my long calls with Scott. My dad and her parents had given me temporary permission to live with her because my dad understood how cramped I was at his apartment.

"Sorry."

"I can't ever talk to my boyfriend, who is a real boyfriend, by the way," she said.

I told Scott we had to keep it to twenty minutes. I wanted him to be satisfied with the phone attention so I didn't have to hang out with him except when we were with Jane and Jimmy. The double-date strategy worked well.

"Movies this weekend?" Jane said as we passed in the hall.

She and I didn't talk on the phone. It was too risky. Her parents were on guard for a relapse. The four of us would meet at the movie theater and Jane and I would go immediately to the ladies' room. If we could get a minute alone, we would kiss and hold each other for as long as we dared. Once I had Jane pressed up against the wall with my hands up her shirt when the door opened and two older women came in. I jumped back and knocked over the trash can, spilling paper towels and Coke cans all over the place.

"I am such a dork!" I said.

They laughed and helped us clean up the mess, so I guess they didn't notice what we were up to. We went on this way for weeks, but then Scott started complaining about not having any time alone.

"Why do we always have to go with Jane and Jimmy? Let's go out by ourselves this weekend."

"I don't know. I don't want to hurt their feelings."

"Jimmy doesn't care. Jane's the one who's obsessed with you."

I was silent for a second, shocked and worried by what he said. "I don't know what you're talking about."

"They say she's a little, you know…squirrely."

I couldn't let him think that. I felt like I had to play along. "First of all, I don't know what you're referring to about Jane. She's crazy over Jimmy. She never stops talking about him. And, okay, just you and me this weekend is great."

I caught Jane outside the girls' locker room during PE and told her I had to go out with Scott alone that weekend.

"What?" she grabbed my wrist and twisted it.

"Ouch!" I said.

"I'm sorry," she said, letting go. "But why?"

"I have to. He thinks there could be something going on with you and me."

"You like him, don't you," she said, pounding her fist against the fence.

"No! I'm just doing this so he shuts up," I said, grasping and holding her hands for way too long.

"What are you going to let him do?"

"Nothing," I said. "Are you kidding?"

I backed away from her, shaking my head.

"He wants to be alone because he wants to get his hands in your pants."

I knew she was right.

"If you won't, he's going to break up with you."

"So what?"

"You can't let him break up with you right before Homecoming. We have to go together."

"That's another three weeks."

"You have to hold him off," she said, gripping my arm. "Even if you're alone with him, you can't let him touch you."

"I won't!"

"I couldn't take it, Cal."

She came really close and I thought she was going to kiss me, but the gym teacher walked by just then.

"Move along, girls," she said, winking.

As the weekend approached, I had less and less stomach for going out with Scott alone and having to fend him off. Then Bev called to say they had information that the gang appeared to be mobilizing for a move into Palo Duro Canyon. There was no indication they were coming back to town, but I should be on the alert. That truly made me sick and I convincingly told Scott I couldn't go out with him that Saturday.

I knew everyone said I had done all I could do for Mom, but it still gnawed at me. I should have been able to save her.

CHAPTER THIRTY-ONE

Homecoming weekend finally arrived. Rachel and Jane helped me shop for a dress since I had no idea how. My mother had always made my clothes. I didn't even know what size I wore. Jane's parents were so excited that she was going to Homecoming with the football captain that they invited Rachel and me to get ready at their house. They brought in a couple of women to do our hair and makeup. And they hired a limo driver who would pick up the boys and bring them over to get us.

We were in Jane's bedroom waiting for her to come out of the dressing area. When she appeared, fully dressed with her hair and makeup done, I thought I would faint. "Oh my gosh," I said. "Look at her, Rachel."

The dress, satin and scarlet red, fit tightly at the waist and cascaded to the floor in a fountain of fabric. Her hair swept up in the back and fastened into a jeweled clip. Rachel whistled. I walked over and got as close as I dared. She smiled at me and I couldn't see anything but her. She and I stood transfixed until Rachel broke in.

"Enough already, you two."

When Rachel and I were ready, we all went downstairs and Jane's parents took so many pictures I thought my face would freeze into a permanent smile. The boys arrived with corsages while we had boutonnieres for them. We all fumbled around trying to get the flowers just right. Jane's mom and the hair and makeup ladies helped us and we took more pictures. Finally, we were off to the high school gym.

Jane and I could not stop looking at each other the whole ride there. Her sleeveless dress framed her shoulders and cut down her chest in a V that took my eye to the curve of her breasts and the space between them. My gaze lingered there a little too long and Rachel nudged me, giving me a wide-eyed look.

When the six of us arrived and stepped out of the limo one by one, we set off a little stir. No one else had arrived in a limo. We walked in, arm in arm with our respective boys, and the night began.

The place was decorated like the bottom of the ocean with shimmering wallpaper, seaweed patches, and floating sharks, dolphins, and other sea creatures. The music pounded and the girls and guys, suddenly shy of each other, separated to opposite sides of the room. There was a rumor that one of the guys had a flask and was handing out shots near the boys' bathroom.

"I'm going," I said. "Are y'all coming?"

They followed me and we all took one.

"Gross! What is that?" Rachel said, making a twisted face.

"Cherry vodka," someone said.

I took another one. Jane whispered to me, "You look so hot in that dress. I'm not sure I can stand to watch you with him all night."

I smiled and teased her, showing off my body in the silky strappy dress that accentuated my chest and hips and scooped low on my breasts. I danced around her, the shots going to my head.

"I'm warning you," she said. "You better stop."

"Okay, fine," I said. "Let's find the guys. We should go ahead and get our official homecoming photo under that flower arch."

As the six of us stood in line, each waiting for the official photo with our date, Jimmy tried to hold Jane's hand. She pushed him away and he grabbed at her waist, pulling her to him.

"Stop," she said. "Don't do that."

"Why not? You're my girlfriend. Act like it."

He slurred his words.

"You're going to mess up my dress," she said. "Just act like a gentleman."

"I don't see why you can't hold my hand," he said, trying again.

She gave in and stood stiffly next to him while he rocked side to side. Watching them, I felt sad and helpless. I wanted to push him out of the way and hold her in my arms. Rachel suddenly popped up between us.

"Hey, let's get an official picture of the six of us together. Homecoming 1973!"

"Thanks," I whispered.

"You two need to cool it," she whispered back.

We stood under the elaborate flower arch the Homecoming committee had built, the boys behind us, their hands, arranged by the photographer, lightly resting on our hips. I glanced at Jane, who did her best to produce a believable smile.

We grazed on the buffet for a while, but the food was terrible. To save money, the Homecoming committee had made it a potluck and by the time we got to it, all the good stuff was gone. I snuck another cherry vodka shot as Rachel, Jane, and I went into the girls' restroom.

I was tipsy enough that I forgot myself and reached for Jane, giving her a silly smile and trying to kiss her. She dodged the kiss and then held me straight-jacket style while fending off the stares of the other girls in the room. Even in my haze, I could tell they were looking at me like I was some kind of alien.

"She's a little drunk," Jane said. "She doesn't know what she's doing."

"Yeah," Rachel chimed in. "She didn't have much to eat. I think maybe we should get her home."

"No!" I said, breaking loose from Jane and forcing my way out of the restroom and back onto the dance floor.

Scott and Jimmy were on the other side of the room with their own alcohol stash. They had Jim Beam and they were pouring it into their Cokes. I reached for Scott's cup, but Jane, suddenly behind me, grabbed my hand.

"You're drunk already," she said.

"C'mon," Scott said, handing me the cup. "Go ahead."

Looking at his outstretched hand, I had trouble focusing. I started to sweat and I felt a little sick to my stomach.

"I better not," I said.

Jane stared at me through slits, her jaw clenched. I wasn't sure what was happening. "Here," she said, handing me a cup of water. "Drink this. You need to slow down."

"I'm fine," I said, but I drank the water.

She stood by my side, keeping an eye on me, to the point that people started to notice. I could tell some of the couples standing near us were talking about us. I turned to Scott, telling him we should get out on the dance floor. Rachel and her boyfriend came out with us.

As the DJ cranked it up with one rock 'n' roll song after another, the dance floor filled and we were all in a pack, no one really paying too close attention to who they were with. I was into it, feeling good again and loose and vaguely aware that Jane wasn't dancing or moving much. She was standing there like a statue. Jimmy was so drunk he didn't notice. He was barely standing at that point. I moved through the crowd to get to her.

"Dance!" I said, pulling at her hand. "Come on, dance with me!"

I couldn't get her to move. She shook her head, her face dark, her expression scornful. I gave up.

"Suit yourself," I said.

The DJ played a slow dance and everyone paired up with their date—except Jane—who stood over at the side. Jimmy was puking into a trash can. I saw Rachel to my right, dancing with her boyfriend, looking into his eyes all goofy. I hadn't realized she was so into him. They were dancing really tight and he had his hands on her butt. An odd feeling flushed through me, like

Rachel had something to herself that I was not a part of. I didn't like it.

Scott pressed up against me, squeezing me around the waist. I felt him against my leg and I could tell he was excited. Then he put his lips on my neck and sucked and I thought, oh, dang, he's going to give me a hickey and what should I do. I tried pulling away, but he held on and got more aggressive. His lips found my mouth and I turned away.

He tried again, but this time I felt someone pushing him away from me. It was Jane. She had pulled the clip out of her hair and it spilled over her face, licking her shoulders like a torrent of wildfire.

"Get the hell away from her!"

She was in his face, shoving him backward across the floor, running into people as she did. I stood there, not moving, watching it happen, not knowing what to do to stop it.

Rachel ran to me. "What is she doing? Has she gone crazy?"

The crowd had moved to the sides of the dance floor, watching as Jane pinned Scott against the wall. I was in a fog, still pretty drunk, staring at the fiasco unfolding.

"We have to get her out of here," Rachel said.

By this time, the music had stopped and the room was eerily quiet as Jane's voice erupted, guttural and animal-like. She still had Scott against the wall as she slapped him on the chest, screaming. "Don't ever touch her again. Do you understand me? I'll kill you!"

Scott stood perfectly still, stunned, saying nothing. I felt like my feet were nailed to the floor. I couldn't move. Jane turned around to face the crowd.

"I don't care what you think! Call me a freak. Call me a homo. Call me queer. I don't care anymore!"

Rachel grabbed my hand and pulled me toward Jane. We got on either side of her, took her arms and moved her as fast as we could out of the crowd and into the hallway. She buried her head on my shoulder and cried like I'd never seen her cry. We tried to go to the girls' restroom, but some of the other girls blocked us. We went outside instead.

I looked around, trying to find the limo driver, but instead, I saw Jane's mother's car speeding into the parking lot and skidding to a stop near the building. *Oh crap. Someone called her.* She jumped out of the car and ran toward us, attacking Jane, slapping her so hard she fell to the ground.

"You disgust me!" she screamed, standing over Jane.

"Please, Mrs. Rawlings," Rachel said, reaching to help Jane.

"And you," she said to me. "You pervert. With your trailer trash mother. I never should have let you near my daughter."

"Get away from me," Jane said, holding the side of her face her mother had bruised. "I don't care about your threats anymore. I'd rather die than be someone I'm not, just so you don't have to be embarrassed."

"Embarrassed?" She laughed. "This is not about me being embarrassed. This is about you ruining your life. Throwing away everything we've given you. Forfeiting your future. Any hope of a family. God knows what will happen to you. There's no place in society for girls like you two."

We stood there staring back at her, saying nothing.

"Do you think you're the first to feel this way?" she went on. "Do you think you're special? Because you're not! But you can't have something just because you want it, just because you feel it. Just because it's all you can think about. Just because every time you close your eyes you imagine your life that way."

Oh my God. Is she talking about herself?

"That's not the way it works," she said. "Not in the real world. Wake up! This is a fantasy." She pointed at me as she said that, but she wasn't finished. "Don't you realize I know what it's like? How do you think I've been so sure about you? But I never thought you would go this far."

I watched Jane. She was amazingly beautiful standing there, tall and defiant.

"I feel sorry for you, Mother. You've lived your life according to a script that someone else wrote," Jane said. "Is that what you want for me? Don't you want me to be happy?"

"You will not be happy if you try to live that life. It's just a phase. Give it some time. You'll forget it."

"You're wrong. This is who I am. And this," she pointed to her dress, "is the last time I'm playing this part. I don't care what you say or do. I will leave home if I have to. But I will be who I am."

She reached for me and pulled me next to her and put both arms around me. I put my arms around her and we stood there under the parking lot lights with Rachel standing behind us with her arms around us both. Mrs. Rawlings looked at us, saying nothing, for what felt like forever, then turned away, walked back to her car, got in and drove away.

"Now what," Rachel said, looking over her shoulder at the crowd that had gathered to gawk at us.

"Can you call your dad?" I asked.

We spent the night at Rachel's. I woke up hungover with a pounding headache. The three of us lay in bed, not one of us making the effort to get up. It was a train wreck. We were forced to stir when Jane's father showed up and asked if she would come out and talk to him. Rachel and I listened at the door.

"Your mother and I talked," he said. "We can't condone this…choice you're making." He paused but Jane said nothing. "We're scared for you. We want the best for you. We love you."

"Dad, I can't—"

"We're not going to fight you anymore. We want a truce."

"You're sure Mom wants me back?"

"It won't be easy. I'm not going to pretend she's not who she is. But whatever you said to her last night hit home somehow. She wants to make it work."

He asked her to come home. She came inside and we hugged her. She kissed me on the lips for a long time.

"I love you," I said. "Good luck."

CHAPTER THIRTY-TWO

The very next night, Rachel and I were sitting in her living room eating TV dinners and watching television when the telephone rang. Rachel went to the kitchen to answer it.

"Cal," she shouted. "Come in here. It's Jane."

"I've got news," Jane said.

"What's going on?" I said.

"Something's happening in the canyon. I know it."

"How do you know?"

"My dad just got picked up by an entourage of Rangers and cops. The gang must have tried something. I don't know what happened, but that has to be why they came for my dad. If they broke into the petroleum reserve, it's his problem."

"Are you thinking what I'm thinking?" Rachel said, looking at me.

"Jane," I said, "how would you feel about—"

"I'll be there in fifteen."

Rachel and I slipped out of her bedroom window and ran down the block to the corner where Jane waited.

"Let's go!" I shouted.

"Plot out a back way, Rachel," I said. "The main entrance will be blocked. I don't know if we can get close, but try to find a remote gate where they might not have guards."

"Are we crazy?" Jane asked, gripping the steering wheel.

"Don't think about it. This could be the final chapter. I want to see it, if I can," I said.

We followed the route Rachel had deciphered, and as we approached the small, dark gate, we noticed a smoldering glow over the horizon. The air had the pungent smell of hot iron and burning embers. Jane took a sledgehammer to the padlock on the gate and opened it so we could drive through.

We drove in the direction of the glow, rolling very slowly, the headlights dark, the dirt road lit by the moonlight and the fire in the sky. When we got as close as we dared, we took out our binoculars.

"It looks like a war zone," Rachel said.

"Is that your dad?" I said to Jane.

"I see him."

Just then, a loud voice splintered my eardrum. "Put your hands in the air!"

We turned to find three Texas Rangers with their guns aimed at our heads. We dropped our binoculars and raised our hands.

"Get moving," one of the Rangers said, pushing us in the direction of the melee.

Mr. Rawlings's eyes were wide with either anger or terror when he saw us being marched into his presence by the Rangers.

"What the—"

"Dad, I can explain," Jane pleaded.

"Get them into that van over there. I'll deal with them."

"Not exactly how I envisioned this," Rachel said as we sat in the police van waiting to find out our fate.

Mr. Rawlings joined us after a while. "Look, girls. I know you think you're Nancy Drew, but this could not be a more dangerous situation. I can't have you here. Jane, I'm really disappointed in you. You know better. I should have you all thrown into the clink to teach you a lesson, once and for all."

"But Dad, what about Cal's mom?"

"Your mom survived, Cal."

We all exhaled loudly and they held my hands.

"But twelve people have died, ten of the conspirators and two law enforcement officers. Many more are injured and are being treated at local hospitals. Your mother is in very serious trouble."

I felt crushed like the weight of a thousand bricks pressed on my chest, cutting off oxygen. The last thing I remember is trying to stand up. When I regained consciousness, Jane and Rachel were crying and pulling me off the floor.

"Get these girls back home," Mr. Rawlings said to the officers.

I don't remember anything about that ride, but the next day, my dad called to offer to drive me to Amarillo to see my mother.

"Can Jane and Rachel come too?"

"Sure," he said. "I'll be over soon."

We arrived in Amarillo just in time for a Texas Rangers press conference.

"Look," Jane said. "There's Bev!"

Bev stood in the background behind the podium on the front steps of the Federal Building.

"Thank goodness she's okay," I said.

A spokesperson for the Texas Rangers took the microphone. "Good morning, ladies and gentlemen. I will make a brief statement and then take questions. Last night at approximately five p.m., members of the Brazos River Gang entered Palo Duro Canyon with the intent to break the security of the Strategic Oil Reserve that, until this attempt, was secretly located there. They met up with members of a syndicate out of Houston to whom they intended to sell access to the Reserve. The Texas Rangers had received a tip that this conspiracy was in motion and had arranged with the FBI to move in on the suspects and subdue them prior to the break-in taking place. When asked to surrender, the suspects opened fire on the Rangers. The FBI moved in with helicopters and counterpunched. At the end of the gun battle, we had lost two of our Rangers. All members of the Brazos River Gang were killed in the encounter. We have in custody a co-conspirator and the surviving members of the Houston syndicate."

"He said they had a tip. That was you!" Jane said.

"It feels weird to hear it."

"You are a hero, Cal," Rachel gushed, clasping her hands together.

"No. I'm no hero."

"I'm so proud of you, Cal," Dad said. "Jane's dad told me the whole story. I had no idea you were so deep in all of this. You were right. It all makes sense now. You are some brave young lady!"

I felt myself blushing. My dad never talked to me like that before. It felt good, but in a strange way.

"Thanks, Dad. It's been a weird few months. In some ways, I feel like all of a sudden I'm an adult. You know what I mean?"

"I do," he said. "You're all grown up."

We had been instructed to go to the FBI field office, where Bev would be waiting for us.

"I wanted to get a minute with you," Bev said, taking me aside. "I want to warn you, the word is getting out that you were the one who tipped us off about the canyon. Not sure how that happened. You're going to get mobbed by press sooner or later. I wouldn't be surprised if they show up here."

"What do I do?"

"Don't say anything. Just look straight ahead and keep walking. We'll have escorts for you and guards until this all calms down."

"And my mom?"

"We're going to take you to see her in a few minutes," Bev said.

"Is she in prison?"

"She's in custody at the Federal Building."

"How is she?"

"She's a little rough. I don't want to scare you, but they have her on suicide watch."

I looked at Dad. I could tell he was still in love with her. He had the worst look on his face. I gave him a hug and told him we would all get through this.

It was a jolt to see my mother sitting behind bulletproof glass in a detention hall. She looked frail and weak. She had lost a lot of weight. She barely glanced up when I walked toward her.

"Come this way," a guard said. "We'll let you be in a room together."

He led us down a hall to a room with a table and a few chairs. My mother had shackles on her ankles with a chain running between them. But her hands were free. We sat across from each other. Her eyes were swollen from crying. She wore no makeup, which made her look younger and more afraid, almost as though part of her armor, her defenses, were wiped away. I was sorry for her, but I was also ready to tear into her.

"Do you have any idea what kind of trouble you're in?" I asked.

It just came out. Daughter to mother. I leaned over, trying to be intimidating. She snapped up and looked at me full in the face for the first time since I got there.

"What do you know about anything? You sit there. Smug. Arrogant. Like you're something special."

"You don't impress me with all that," I said. "I just want to know why you did it."

Somebody had left a pack of cigarettes on the table with some matches. She lit one and we sat there in silence while she took a couple of drags.

"I don't owe you any explanation," she said, "but I am going to tell you a few things because you think you know everything, but you don't."

I sat back and waited.

"I married your dad the week after I graduated high school because I had to get out of my momma and daddy's house. Daddy wouldn't leave me alone. And I know you know what I mean. That's why my mother threw him out. I'm sure you've wondered about that."

I felt a rush of disgust wash over me. I had only vague memories of my grandfather. He had drifted away when I was much younger and no one seemed to know what became of him. What she told me now made me feel sick.

"Daddy had started in on me when I was twelve. If I hadn't gotten out when I did, I think I would have killed myself. And I didn't see any other way out besides marrying someone and setting up my own house. So I picked your dad. He was a year ahead of me. Had a good job. Seemed nice enough. So that was that."

As she painted this picture, I began to think of my parents in a way I never had before. When you don't know any better, you don't think about it. But I realized my mother and father had never paid attention to each other in front of me in any way other than two people with a list of things to do. I couldn't remember them hugging or kissing. I suddenly felt deeply sorry for both of them.

"The years went by. You were born. He and I came and went without so much as a hello some days. I was empty. My life stretched out in front of me like a desert with no life in sight."

She paused to suck on the cigarette. "Then I met him."

She stood up, turned her back and held herself together, gripping her arms in a hunched-over hug.

"The first time I ever saw him, I knew. This was it. This was the man I had been waiting for. He was my destiny."

My mouth went dry and I started to sweat, as though her words had turned the heat up in the room. I was desperate for a drink of water.

"The way he treated me, no one ever treated me like that before. Paid me that much attention. Told me I was beautiful. Told me I was his everything. Told me he would take care of me. I was a princess. There was nothing we couldn't do together. No challenge we couldn't handle."

She changed in front of me as she talked about him—from a broken, empty, hopeless shell to a fierce and intimidating woman. I stood to balance the energy between us.

"Well, that's all just great," I said, folding my arms, "but why did you have to go along with this giant scheme? Didn't you understand how wrong it was?"

She stubbed her cigarette out in the ashtray on the table. "I knew it was wrong, but I would have done anything to be with him."

"How were you going to get away with it?"

"We had the one last heist. The big one. With that, we were going away. We were going to start over."

"And what about me?"

"You've always been strong. You didn't need me. Not really. I knew you'd be fine. I had to take my chance when it came. I would do it again. I couldn't go back to who I was before I met him."

My mother didn't care how all of this affected me. Not one bit. I couldn't look at her anymore.

"I hid some money for you," she said.

"I don't want that money," I said.

"You deserve a good start in life. What difference does it make where it came from?"

"Just forget it. I'm not taking any money from you."

"Well, that's just like you. You think you're better than me, but you're not. You're from the same line. Don't think the time won't come when you're tempted to do something that you know is wrong. You'll rationalize it. Just like everybody else."

I couldn't listen to any more of it.

"Good luck to you, Mother. You'll need it."

CHAPTER THIRTY-THREE

There was one more thing I had to do before I could leave Amarillo. I had to be interviewed by the Texas Rangers. Bev went with me and introduced me to a man in a very fancy uniform. "I'm Commander Morris," he said. We shook hands and he invited me to sit down. "I've heard quite a lot of good things about you."

"Thank you, sir."

"What you did, the information you got for us, you realize you're a very brave young woman."

"I don't know about that..."

"There's something I want to talk to you about. Make sure you understand."

He paused. "Your mother is going to be charged with some very serious crimes."

"I understand."

"And you are a key witness to some of those crimes."

I nodded.

"How do you feel about helping us make the case against your mother?"

"Do I really have a choice?"

"We can compel you to testify against her. But I would rather have your cooperation. It will be more effective."

I thought about it, but not for long. "I'll tell you the truth. I'll tell you everything I know. That's what I have to do. If it means she goes to prison, there's nothing I can do about that."

"I just wanted to be sure," he said. "I know it must be very hard."

"She did what she did. It was her free will. She doesn't regret it. She may be my mother, but that doesn't change what happened and what I have to do."

"Very good, then," he said. "We will be in touch."

Bev and I left the building and she stopped me at the top of the stone stairs.

"Are you sure about what you said in there?"

"I don't think I could live with myself if I stayed silent. I tried as hard as I could to get her to leave him. To just walk away. She wouldn't do it. She told me she would have done anything for him. So now, if she goes to prison for him, well, maybe it's what she wants."

My mother's trial was set for a few weeks later. She had refused to cooperate with the prosecution of the Houston contingent, so they were going after her for the maximum sentence. They told me she wanted to take her punishment. She didn't want to get off easy at someone else's expense. I felt oddly proud of her for that.

We all three testified, though Rachel and Jane were much less important to the prosecution. Jane was first to take the stand. She answered every question as simply as possible, not offering any extra detail, and keeping her eyes on me in between. I sent her imaginary hugs and kisses, knowing how hard it was for her to say things that would help send my mother to prison.

When Rachel took the stand, she was so excited I thought she might jump into the jury box. She looked at them for their reaction to every answer she gave, convinced, I'm sure, that her testimony was the key to the case. When the prosecutor asked her to point out my mother and identify her, she looked at me smugly as she mimicked what we'd heard on *Perry Mason* a hundred times. I covered my ears as she delivered her answer with a dramatic flair fit for television.

When my turn came, it was much harder than I'd thought. With every answer, I wanted to offer an explanation. I wanted the jury to understand why she did what she did.

"I know it sounds bad," I said, looking at them in their box, "but she's not a bad person. She—"

"Please, Miss Long, just answer the question," the prosecutor said.

Her defense attorney gave me the chance. He asked me to describe what she was like as a mother.

"Up until she met...that man, Hank Hart, she was always there for me. She made all my clothes. We always had dinner together. She took good care of me."

My mother looked up at me as I said that. She was so small, sitting behind the defense counsel's table. I saw a tear slip down her cheek.

The jury wasn't out very long before they came back with the verdict. Rachel and Jane and I held hands as the foreman read it out loud. They found her guilty. The only question was the sentence and that would come later.

So just like that, it was all over.

A few weeks later, Jane drove me to Amarillo, to the courtroom, to see her sentenced. They went easier on her than I thought. She might be out in a few years with good behavior. Afterward, I asked if I could speak to her. They took me to a side chamber off the courtroom.

"I wanted to say goodbye for now, Mom."

She looked up and I realized we hadn't seen eye to eye for a long time. She was beaten down, defeated, older.

"I'm sorry," she said. "You deserved better than this."

I didn't know what to say.

"I put him first. Nothing else, no one else mattered. What I did was wrong. And I knew it. And I didn't care."

She paused but didn't take her eyes off me.

"Try to forget me."

"I won't...I can't forget."

"I'm sorry, miss," the guard said. "We have to go now."

I nodded. And suddenly, I couldn't stop myself. I hugged her, tears slipping out and down my face. "I love you, Mom. Take care of yourself."

She kept her eye on me until the guard had walked her through the door.

I sat next to Jane as she drove us away from Amarillo. She had her hand on my thigh. The flat, empty, dry landscape stretched out in front of us as far as we could see.

"I think I understand her a little," I said.

"Tell me."

"It's sort of like what you said."

"What do you mean?"

"About the script of your life. She met someone who threw out the script, who changed everything. And even though it meant breaking every rule she'd lived by up until then, she did it anyway because of love. Can you imagine a love like that?"

"Yes, I can," she said, holding my hand. "Yes, I can."

Bella Books, Inc.

Women. Books. Even Better Together.

P.O. Box 10543
Tallahassee, FL 32302

Phone: 800-729-4992
www.bellabooks.com

CPSIA information can be obtained
at www.ICGtesting.com
Printed in the USA
BVHW071936280519
549516BV00001B/44/P